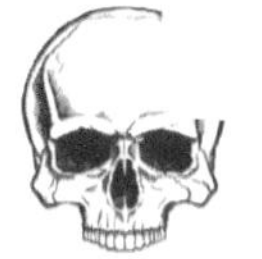

THE FOURTH CORONA BOOK OF HORROR STORIES

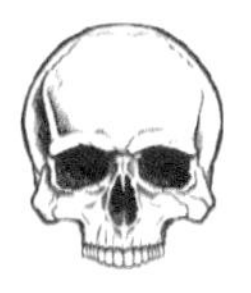

THE FOURTH CORONA BOOK OF HORROR STORIES

edited by
LEWIS WILLIAMS

First published in the United Kingdom in 2022

by Corona Books UK
www.coronabooks.com

ISBN 978-1-9996579-6-3

Cover design by Martin Bushell
www.creatusadvertising.co.uk

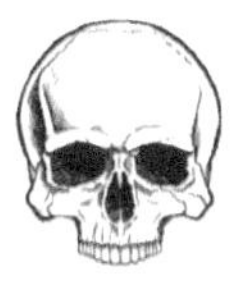

CONTENTS

INTRODUCTION

Everything was going pretty well for Corona Books back at the beginning of 2020. We'd just published *The Third Corona Book of Horror Stories* which had attracted over 800 submissions from authors wanting their stories to appear in it; and finally after years of trying we'd managed to secure a face-to-face meeting with Waterstones, the UK's largest bookstore chain, who agreed to stock our books in a number of their shops nationwide. And then… well, to paraphrase Bruce Springsteen, there are some things you don't even see coming that can knock you down. Along came a virus that alas shared our name and made it virtually impossible to try and promote ourselves without attracting criticism or ridicule. The nicer of the comments we were getting at the time said things like, 'Do you get a free virus with that book?' and the nastier comments accused us of trying to cash in on the virus that was then in the process of killing people – which of course we weren't, having started publishing in 2015 long before the pandemic became a thing. With heavy hearts we felt had to take the decision to put the publication of any new titles on hold. So, no new Corona Books titles appeared in 2020 or 2021, and our plans to publish *The Second Corona Book of Science Fiction* and *The Fourth Corona Book of Horror Stories* in particular were put on ice.

The global pandemic turned out to be awful in so many ways for all of us, I know, and to keep things in perspective we didn't lose anybody at Corona Books to the virus or anything like that, but the cancellation of these titles was a disappointment to me and to the authors we'd had lined up to have their stories included in them. In 2019 I'd been going round happily telling anyone who'd listen that as long as my heart was still beating there'd be a Corona Book of Horror Stories published every year from now on whatever happened. It wasn't to be.

However, now that the Corona name is hopefully going to be a lot less toxic than it was proving to be back in early 2020, we are publishing the book you have before you. Are we picking up exactly as we left off three years ago? Yes and no. Yes, we remain fiercely independent and 100% committed to publishing the best in new horror writing from the genuinely brilliant wealth of talent out there that mainstream publishers are apt to ignore. Nothing has changed there, but *The Fourth Corona Book of Horror Stories* differs from its predecessors (and from the book it probably would have been in 2020) in a couple of ways. Firstly, with a total of 20 entries, it has more stories in it than any of the other anthologies we've published before. Secondly, it includes both some stories that are, I think, darker in tone than anything we've published before and some stories that are, I think, lighter in tone than anything we've published before.

To put things another way, with this volume we're offering more in the way of quantity and more in the way of variety than we've done before, but quality remains an ever-present constant.

So, depending on your choice of metaphor, strap yourself in for a memorable rollercoaster ride or prepare to indulge yourself in a tantalising selection box – and forgive me for having the nerve to include a story of my own within the contents, albeit a very short one indeed.

In this book, as with all our other anthologies, we've chosen to preserve the authors' native version of English spelling, punctuation and grammar. This is out of respect for our authors' creations and to avoid the strangeness that would ensue from Anglicising stories with an American setting or Americanising stories with a British setting were we to insist on everything being in British English or alternatively everything being in American English. So, the stories by the five American authors (MM Schreier, Sam Rebelein, Vanessa Reid, Florence Ann Marlowe and Wondra Vanian) included in this collection appear in American English; the story by the one Canadian author (Jon Gauthier) appears in Canadian English; and the stories by the two Australian authors (Deborah Sheldon and Justin Cawthorne) appear in Australian English.

Elsewhere the book is presented in British English (where we have fibres, colours and centres rather than fibers, colors and centers etc.) Although sometimes subtle, the differences in the different versions of English extend to punctuation too. For example, in American English the use of double quotes is favoured for speech, whereas we Brits, it seems, prefer single quotes when it comes to fiction in print. And in American English certain punctuation marks appear inside quotes that it wouldn't be correct for them to do so in British English. These differences are not mistakes!

Also as with all our other anthologies, in case of interest and to aid readers who might want to check out other writing from the authors of their favourite stories in the book, at the end of the book we've included brief biographies of all the contributors along with a listing of Twitter accounts and author websites for those that have them.

Now without further ado, on with the (horror) show!

Lewis Williams
Withernsea, Summer 2022

HERE PIGGY, PIGGY

Florence Ann Marlowe

The road leading up to the witch's house was a dark and lonely one. Cody kicked at a can lying in the gravel as he and the other two young men trudged through the brush. Vinnie jumped a foot and hissed at him, "What the fuck's the matter with you? We're trying to keep a low profile here!"

"Aw, shut the fuck up," Cody muttered. "Nobody's around. Nobody can hear us."

"That's not the fucking point, Cody." Vinnie trotted up to Cody's side. "We're trying to take advantage of the element of surprise here."

Cody grinned. Vinnie could be such an asshole: twenty-three and still playing video games in his head. "The surprise comes from what we're <u>not</u> going to do, Vinnie, not what we're <u>gonna</u> do."

"What the fuck does that mean?" A dog barked somewhere in the distance and Vinnie jumped again.

"It means we're not going to pay her." Cody took another swipe at the can with his foot and missed. "The witch expects to get paid, but we ain't got the cash, so we got to keep that our little secret."

Jonah gave the can a kick as he caught up with Vinnie and Cody. "Yeah, but what if she figures us out?" He glanced around at the fields, heavy with produce so late in the summer. "What kind of witch is she anyway? What kind of witch lives on a farm?"

Cody expelled an exasperated sigh. It was difficult being the only intellect in his circle of friends. He felt he had been carrying both Vinnie and Jonah since high school. He was always the brains, always the leader. He was the one who had to get them into trouble and to figure a way to get them out of it again.

"The bitch is an honest-to-God witch, like the old lady in the Harry Potter movies. Since I was a kid I've seen assholes pay her for love potions and candles and shit like that," Cody said. "All the other farms in Morgan County are going under, but she manages to keep going. How you figure she's done that?"

Vinnie shrugged. "Maybe she comes from a farming family."

"Yeah, like the Mulhaneys? Look what happened to them," Cody snickered.

"Does the old lady have a dog, Cody?" Jonah asked as they rounded the path and saw the old A-frame farm house.

Cody shook his head. "She's no old lady. She's my mom's age. They actually went to school together."

The three young men stopped in front of the picket fence surrounding the property. Sunflowers bobbed on their six-foot stems from the front yard. There was a stone lying in front of a small patch of grass by the gate. The name "Jo-jo" was painted on the stone in faded blue letters. Years ago, the witch had had a dog. Cody remembered killing it with his pellet gun after she had caught him teasing her pigs. His father had beat him with his belt for that. Willie Patterson always had a soft spot for the witch, for some odd reason.

"Okay, let me do all the talking here. We're going to explain what we want without letting on that we haven't got any money, you dig?"

Vinnie nodded and Jonah sighed before silently agreeing. They stepped up the wooden porch and Cody rapped on the door.

Cora Lee Sullivan had lived in the old farm house since she was born. Her family had raised pigs and chickens and planted corn and other crops for over a hundred years. She had carried on when her father died in '89 and had lived alone save for animal companionship, tending her fields and selling produce to the local grocers. She was also known as the local witch. She answered the door and looked back at the three boys with some surprise.

"Cody? Cody Patterson, what are you doing here so late? It's nine PM."

Cody had to think for a moment what the appropriate response might be. Cody didn't remember her being so attractive. When he was in high school she'd been heavier, draped in baggy muumuus, chasing him and his brother Roy with a rake when they rode their bikes through her watermelon patch. The dark-haired woman peering back at him from behind her front door looked younger than her mid-forties, her eyes a deep indigo blue that seemed shocking in the bright hallway light. He'd expected a pale, pasty-looking thing, but her skin was tawny from working in the sun and her lips were full and red, like ripe fruit.

A smile spread across Cody's face. "Relax, Cora, this is

important. The guys and me have a job for you."

Cora looked over the other two and then opened the door wide, beckoning them to enter. The living room was warm and familiar, nothing like Cody had envisioned. He had expected to see apothecary jars and bottles of toads and mice floating in viscous fluid. The room was a haze of comfortable browns and beiges; the TV was on, the sound muted.

"What kind of job could you possibly have for me, Cody?" Cora was wearing what Cody's mother would call a "house dress." Big yellow flowers made up deep pockets on the front of the blue cotton garment. She folded her legs under her as she sat on the worn sofa and clicked the television off with the remote.

A little shaken by Cora's bluntness, Cody glanced at his friends before beginning his pitch. "We've got a problem with some guy in town who stuck his nose where it doesn't belong. He needs to be taught a lesson."

Cora simply stared back at the young man.

"He got mixed up with my girlfriend. She's with him now and—well, I don't think she's really happy. He's kind of controlling her."

"Would this guy in town be Ricky Moore?" Cora asked.

Cody blinked and Vinnie let out a noisy sigh. "Yeah. How the hell do you know?"

Cora shrugged. "I'm guessing that your girlfriend— Denise Millhouse? I'm guessing she decided to be with him after he intervened when you slapped her around in front of Fusco's Deli."

"Shit," Jonah muttered.

Cody was dumbfounded.

Cora sat back and shook her head. "You shouldn't bully people in public, Cody. People talk. Frieda Fusco told everyone who came into her store how Ricky stopped you from beating up that poor girl."

Cody felt a curl of anger unfold in his chest. "Fuck that! He shouldn't have been sticking his nose in other people's business!"

Cora nodded. "Now why would a big, strong boy like you need my help to teach Ricky a lesson?"

Cody squared his shoulders. He hadn't expected to be interrupted so early in his presentation. "He needs being taken down a peg." He pointed his finger at Cora, cautioning her to understand his meaning. "That asshole thinks he's better than everybody else. He got Vinnie fired from the body shop!" Cody swung his finger in Vinnie's direction. The boy flinched and then nodded reluctantly.

"And Jonah got burned when he was playing for the Ravens," Cody continued. "He got kicked off the team 'cause of Ricky."

Cora raised an eyebrow. "But how do you plan to punish him?"

Suddenly unsure of himself, Cody shrugged. "Hey, I know you've got things you can do. You got spells and stuff." He looked back at Vinnie and Jonah. Silent, they averted their eyes, studying the bric-a-brac on Cora's living room walls. "Maybe you can have something happen to him. Make him sick. Not real bad, just bad enough to make him sorry."

The smile Cora gave him made that curl of anger in Cody's chest twitch. "What makes you think I can do that to someone?"

"Aw, c'mon! Everybody knows you made that old bitch Mrs. Finch get sick last summer."

The smile slipped from Cora's calm face.

"She wanted your pig pen closed up. Said it stunk up the whole town. And next thing you know, the bitch is puking up blood, can't even walk. Everybody knows you did it to her."

Cora shook her head. "I don't do black magic. You need to use black forces to impose hurt on another human being and there's always a price to pay. Nobody's worth that—not even that sourpuss."

Cody shoved his hands into his jean pockets. "We can pay." From behind him, Jonah made a retching sound.

"What a child. You can't afford any such thing, Cody." Cora folded her hands in her lap. "I won't help you hurt Ricky or anyone else. You'll have to find some other way to get back at him for protecting your girlfriend."

The curl unraveled into a great furl of rage. This wasn't going as he'd planned, at all, and he was getting no help from his two mute friends. Cody pulled balled-up fists from his pockets. His shoulders were trembling.

"You were always a mean little boy, Cody. I can remember when you were only eight years old, throwing rocks at my chickens and later, when you were older, setting off firecrackers to scare my horses. You're just mad you can't hurt Ricky with your own two fists." She leaned forward. "Did your daddy get you all riled up over this, Cody? Your father was always a vindictive bastard. Did he tell you, you had to take care of Ricky?"

At the mention of his father, something broke free in Cody's tightly wound chest.

"Listen, you cunt! You don't know shit about my

father!" Cody lunged forward, making Cora flinch.

"I know your daddy very well, Cody." Cora recovered quickly. "He and I fucked in high school."

Cody's arm swung back and his palm met Cora's sunburned cheek with a loud flat slap. Jonah jumped, colliding with the buffet, rattling the ceramic figures displayed on top. Vinnie let out a girlish shriek.

The sensation of flesh on flesh was intoxicating to Cody. "You fucking sow!" He felt his father's voice creep into his mouth. He'd seen his father slap his mother and call her those exact words many times since he was a kid. "You fucking talk to me like I'm some kind of asshole? You think I'm an asshole?" He slapped her again, knocking her back on the couch.

"Jesus fucking Christ, Cody!" Vinnie screamed from behind him. Jonah's hand was clamped over his mouth, his eyes lidless with shock.

"Get out!" Cora shrieked, shielding her face with her arms. "Get out of my house!" The terror in her voice thrilled Cody. He pounced on her, grabbing her arms and pinning them over her head. His face was pressed close to hers.

"Vinnie! Gimme a hand!" Cody heard the slam of the screen door. He glanced up and saw the hallway door swung wide open, the screen door still banging against the jamb. His friends had taken off.

Cora tried to push him off her, but Cody slammed her shoulders onto the couch. He brought up one knee onto her lap.

"You fucking bitch! You wanna see what a little boy I am? Fucking witch!" He grabbed at her dress and it tore away from her shoulder. He pulled it down, exposing her white breasts. Her nipples were bright pink pebbles. He reached out and slapped at her vulnerable tits.

"Fucking sow!" He tore the rest of her dress from her body. It hung at her waist. Cora let out a raw scream that ended in a sob. He forced her over onto her stomach and wrenched what was left of her garment off her hips. She scrabbled for the floor, but Cody grabbed her by the hair and bent her over the back of the sofa. He tore at his belt and ripped open his fly. His erection was enormous. Cora's shrieks filled his head like the green scent of weed.

The fury of his need mounted inside him until he thought he was going to explode. His face seemed on fire. The whiteness of her bare back, the outline of her farmer's tan ending where a short-sleeved T-shirt would block the sun, seemed unbearably real to Cody. Her voice, raw with panic, was hoarse as she repeatedly screamed, "No, no!"

Cody's hand was tangled in her dark hair. He could feel her sides bellowing beneath him as she panted. For a few moments, the realization of what he was about to do spread over Cody in small waves of understanding and dread. His cock was still in his other hand, pointed at Cora's exposed ass. For a moment he thought of his father's pistol. Letting go of Cora's hair, Cody stepped away from the couch. Cora crumpled onto the sofa, sobbing. As he buckled his belt, he was aware that the room was uncomfortably silent.

Cora wedged herself into a corner of the sofa. She looked small in the remains of her house dress. A yellow flower that had once been a pocket dangled by a thread from the garment. Cora pulled a fuzzy crocheted afghan off the back of the sofa into her lap and unfolded it. With agonizing slowness, she began to wrap it around her shoulders, covering her naked breasts with it. Cody watched her chest heave with each silent sob.

The sound of tires on the gravel driveway outside brought Cody back to reality and he turned towards the door. The flash of emergency lights washed the living room in crimson color. Cody heard the sound of two car doors slamming and then the crunch of boots on gravel drawing closer to the house.

"Miz Sullivan?" one of the police officers called as he rapped on the door frame with his flashlight.

Cody turned to look at Cora and muttered under his breath, "Watch it."

But Cora was smiling. "Bobby? Is that you?"

"Officer Poole, Ma'am. We got a phone call that someone was under attack in here."

Fucking Jonah, Cody thought bitterly. And fucking Bobby Poole. Poole graduated the year before Cody and had gone straight to the police academy. He was always a big-ass hero in his own mind. Now he was going to bust Cody.

"Bobby, how's your dad?" Cora had pulled the afghan closer to her chest. She brushed her hair back from her face and smiled.

"He's fine, Miz Sullivan. How are you doing?" Poole glanced over at Cody.

"I'm fine, sweetie. Cody and I were just having a little visit."

The other officer was Dean Torres, who had been in Cody's class. He nodded to Cody. "Where's your car, Cody?"

Cody didn't blink. "It's home. Carburetor's shot."

"So you're gonna be needing a ride home," Torres said. Poole nodded and glanced at his partner.

"Oh, no need," Cora said. "I was just telling Cody he could borrow my pickup until he gets his car fixed."

Poole studied Cora's placid face. "Are you sure you're all right, ma'am?"

Cora laughed and nodded. "I'm fine, Bobby. We're all fine. I'm just a tad tired."

Poole seemed satisfied and nodded. Cora motioned to the buffet. "The keys are in that green cup, Cody. It's on the side of the house. Just watch my herb garden when you pull out."

Cody moved like a wooden soldier towards the buffet and fished the keys out of the cup.

"And you can bring it back tomorrow, Cody," Cora continued. "Say around eight PM?" Her dark blue eyes met Cody's and he nodded in agreement.

Poole moved aside so Cody could get past him. The police officer's gaze never left the young man's face and Cody could feel it burning into his skull.

At seven thirty the following evening, Cody rolled Cora Sullivan's beat-up blue pickup truck down the gravel driveway and left it in front of her garage. He noticed the hall light click on as he slammed the truck door shut. There was a chill in the late-August night air and Cody pulled the sleeves of his chambray shirt down, buttoning the cuffs. He kept his gaze fixed on Cora's front door, expecting it to fly open at any moment with Cora standing in its frame, lifting a shotgun to her shoulder. The door remained closed as he mounted the porch steps.

He didn't knock before entering. Cora was lighting candles. Her dining room table, the sideboard and the coffee table all had long white tapers lit, giving the room a warm, ethereal glow. Cora was dressed in a slim black sheath of a dress, a gauzy red shawl wrapped around her shoulders. Cody took note of a bright red spot on her cheekbone where he'd struck her the night before.

Smiling, Cora turned towards Cody. Her eyes were a deep violet in the candlelight. "What's the matter, Cody?" She blew out her match and rounded the sofa. Cody could clearly see the outline of her body beneath the thin material of her dress. "You look like a goose walked over your grave."

"What the fuck was that last night?" It was uncomfortably warm in the dim-lit room and he began to unbutton his shirt sleeves.

Cora curled up on the sofa. A pair of wine flutes and a bottle of unopened Chianti sat on the coffee table amid the cluster of candles.

"That shit you gave Poole last night? What the fuck was that?" he demanded.

"Cody,"—Cora's voice was like velvet—"haven't you ever been told that some women like it rough?"

Cody raised an eyebrow.

"You really surprised me last night. I didn't realize what a man you've become."

"Bullshit." The young man's voice was edged with uncertainty.

"You really are your father's son," Cora purred as she opened the bottle of Chianti. "You're strong, athletic, powerful—good shot with a pellet gun."

She poured full glasses of the wine as she spoke. Cody's fists were clenched, but he could feel his shoulders beginning to relax.

"You're shitting me," he said. "You're fucking telling me you <u>liked</u> what I did to you?" The taint of disgust crept into his voice.

"It's been a long time since I felt like that, Cody. It gets lonely up here, all by myself." She lifted a glass and offered it to him. Cody snorted and sat next to her on the couch. The glass felt cold in his hand.

"Like you couldn't put a spell on some guy to do what you wanted him to do," Cody snickered. He glanced at the tiny bubbles dissipating on the surface of the contents of his glass and then looked up at Cora.

"It doesn't work like that, Cody." She sipped her wine, her eyes steady on his face. Her smile was benign. She ran her tongue over her full lips and Cody felt something stir in his groin.

"There's no potion to make a woman feel that kind of heat between her legs," Cora said. "I might as well buy myself a vibrator." She laughed and took a long swallow from her glass. "You're a strong man with a big dick, Cody. No potion or spell can duplicate that."

Cody drained his glass in two gulps. The wine was dry. It tasted like ginger ale to him. "So there's nothing you can cook up to make you cum like I can?" He grinned, feeling more sure of himself. The witch was hot for him, he could feel it. She smelled like sunflowers, warm and heady. It reminded him of walking the back roads through the fields on a hot summer day.

Cora shook her head and set her glass down. "No

witchcraft can make you cum or make you fall in love."

Cody sneered.

"There are things that can make your erections harder, last longer," she admitted.

"Like Viagra?" Cody grabbed the neck of the bottle and poured himself another drink. He topped up Cora's glass as well.

"Better than Viagra." Cora moved to the buffet and began to rifle through one of the drawers. She produced a yellow plastic jar the size of a can of peanuts.

"This salve takes the desire already inside you and heats it up. Your own sex drive is multiplied until it builds up like a pressure cooker. It produces tremendous hard-ons and the ejaculation is incredible. I sell hundreds of jars of this stuff, especially around Valentine's Day."

Cody regarded the plastic container before taking it from Cora's hand. It was heavy for its size. He turned the lid and studied the thick white cream inside. It smelled like bacon.

"What's in it?" He sniffed at the contents.

"Herbs, lanolin, olive oil, lard. A few secret things." Her eyes glittered like twin stones of amethyst.

"So what do I do? Rub it on my cock?"

Cora laughed and took the jar from Cody. "I don't think it would be a good idea to let *you* use this."

Cody motioned with his hands. "Give it to me."

She shook her head. "You've already got a pretty powerful sex drive. This could be dangerous."

"Fuck that. Gimme." He reached for the container, but she held it close to her chest.

"You use it like massage oil. Open your shirt."

Cody unbuttoned his shirt and watched as Cora spread some of the cream on his chest and neck. He immediately felt a luscious warmth run up his shoulders.

"Damn!" He pulled his shirt wide open.

Cora dipped her fingers into the container again and rubbed more on his stomach. Cody pulled the shirt off and tossed it aside. The heat ran into his groin and nestled behind his balls. There was a kickback that he felt spreading down his thighs.

Cora was using both hands now, massaging the cream into his shoulders and down his arms. Cody's penis throbbed. He whipped open his belt and fought to free his cock, which seemed to be straining against the zipper, threatening to break free. Cora's hands rubbed the cream into his hips, over his buttocks and into the flesh of his thighs. Cody could feel his muscles vibrating beneath her hot palms. They seemed to stretch and ripple on their own. He began to thrust his hips forward. Glancing down, he could see his erect cock practically standing parallel to his body. It looked huge and purple, engorged with blood.

"HOLY FUCKING SHIT!" he roared, his pants falling to his ankles. Cora's head was between his legs now, her hair tickling his thighs as she continued massaging his calves and feet with the salve. She drew her hands up his legs, his waist, catching his shoulders from behind. She gently lowered him back onto the sofa, her face fixated on his own.

Cody was moaning, deep guttural sounds escaping his throat as he penetrated the air with his cock. Cora's hands felt like flames fluttering up and down his flesh. She grasped his face in her hands and rubbed more of the cream into his cheeks, his neck, even his hair. Cody lurched forward, his mouth searching for her lips. She pushed him back, her palms stroking his face, her fingers running down the bridge of his nose to his lips. Cody's eyes locked with hers and he could hear her whispering softly.

"Here, piggy, piggy."

Over his own lustful panting, Cody was unsure of what he was hearing.

"Here, piggy, piggy." Cora's silky voice was growing in volume.

She took her thumb and placed it beneath his nose. She flicked his nose up and back, pushing it nearly flat against his face, exposing his nostrils. Cody gasped and tried to grab her arm, but the heat in his arms seemed to have turned to liquid. His limbs were rubbery and wouldn't move.

Cora grabbed Cody's cheeks and squeezed. There was no pain, but Cody felt the flesh swell. She shook the two handfuls of flesh and rolled them about. Then, releasing her grip, Cora slapped Cody's face on one cheek. His head rocked back and he felt the odd sensation of floating. She then slapped his other cheek. Round globs of fat hung from his face in the form of great jowls. Cody was stunned.

Cora then took a handful of the oily-smelling salve and rubbed it on Cody's throat, smoothing it down his chest to his stomach. Her hands moved quickly, rolling his flesh about. Cody glanced down and could see the skin expanding, becoming elastic. His stomach began to rise and swell like a ball of yeast bread. He watched as his bellybutton disappeared into the rising mound.

"Here piggy, piggy, piggy," Cora sang as she grabbed the monstrous mountain of flesh that had been Cody's stomach and spread it around with her hands, rolling it onto his hips. It enveloped his torso, swallowing his arms and legs. She slapped at it, sliding her palms up and down his body as if she were molding clay. Too paralyzed to do anything else, Cody found his voice.

"Stop! Leave it!"

Cora ignored his shouts and grabbed his face, buried in pounds of excessive flesh. Cody could barely see over his own cheeks. She rubbed more salve into his hair, her hands massaging his scalp. Tendrils of Cody's sun-bleached blond hair began to drift down before his eyes. She kneaded his scalp, gathering up the growing flesh and rolling it between her palms like a ball of dough.

Cody realized he was sobbing now, tears leaking into the folds of his newly renovated face. Cora stopped to peer into his swollen visage and she smiled. Her forefingers met in the middle of his brow and she traced them away from each other, out to his ears. She took each ear between her fingers and pinched them.

"Here, piggy, piggy."

The tips of his ears caught between her fingers; Cody felt them stretch. Cora pulled them up and away, drawing them out into huge flaps that even a Ferengi would envy. She tweaked them a bit and then pulled them forward. With what little peripheral vision Cody had left he could see them hanging on either side of his face.

She then plucked at Cody's nipples and shook them like teabags. He felt a twinge where she gripped the tender skin. The flesh beneath each nipple billowed and grew. She released the nipple and drew both hands together around his breasts.

"Here, piggy, piggy."

Dragging the flesh upward she rolled them in her hands, thrusting them out and back against his chest. With each thrust, Cody felt a pinch between his breasts. She did this four times and finally released the bruised mammaries. In their place were four more nipples surrounded by a mound of fat, a total of six swollen tits.

Howling, Cody tried to struggle. Sensation was slowly returning to his body, but he still had no control over his limbs. His mouth couldn't form the words he wanted to say. "Bitch," "Cunt," and "Fuck" all were expelled in throaty grunts.

Cora grabbed Cody by the back of his now thick neck and pulled him forward. He lay across her lap in a bulky lump. With the flat of her hand Cora began to slap his buttocks over and over. With each impact his buttocks swelled and grew in size until they were gelatinous orbs of fat hanging off his frame. She reached between his buttocks, just above his anus and used her thumb and forefinger to pinch away a bit of skin. It stretched into a long ribbon of flesh about eight inches long. Cora wrapped it around her finger in a coil and then released it. It sprung back in the shape of a perfect corkscrew.

She flung him onto his back on the couch and stood over him. From his fleshy prison, Cody's arms and legs stuck out, stubby and useless. Cora stripped Cody's tube socks off and began to massage his feet between her hands. Cody felt his toes disappear into the flesh, melded into one big appendage. He sobbed as she did the same to his hands, rolling them into plump little stumps.

Lying on his back, Cody paddled the air with his shortened limbs. He continued to shout, but his voice was garbled. He watched Cora study him, her hands poking at his body, adjusting folds of fat, plumping cushions of flesh as it suited her. She pinched one of his six nipples and watched him flinch.

"Getting some feeling back, Cody?"

A strangled noise escaped his throat. He'd meant it to be a threat.

Cora nodded. She bent low, between Cody's legs, and reached for his penis, still stout and erect. A string of angry bleats issued from Cody's mouth. Cora latched onto his cock and pushed it deep into his groin. He could feel it penetrate his body cavity. She shoved it deeper, her arm disappearing into his torso up to her elbow. Cody's mutilated legs flailed the air. Cora's arm reappeared and she stood back.

The witch regarded her handiwork for a moment. She cocked her head to one side, her dark hair falling in front of her face. She raised one finger and left Cody writhing on the sofa. She returned with a pair of garden shears.

"You won't need these anymore."

Before Cody realized what she was about to do, the loud snick of the blades neatly removed his testicles without a trace of blood. She juggled them in her hand before dropping them into the green cup on the buffet.

Cody bellowed. His cries ended in throaty sobs. All four limbs beat at the air as he tried to stand up. His body was too round and flabby to turn himself upright.

Cora slipped off her shoes and reached under the sofa and produced a pair of mucking boots. She slid them onto her feet and rolled Cody onto the floor. He squealed over and over again as she gathered him up into her arms like a massive sack of potatoes and carried him out the front door and down to the pig pen.

* * *

Two weeks later Officer Poole showed up at Cora's door. She had just finished spreading manure in the fallow fields. She hopped off her John Deere and swiped at the sweat on her face.

"Hey Bobby. What's going on?"

Poole was carefully making his way past the pig pen, trying to avoid both mud and horse shit. "Miz Sullivan, I just wanted to follow up with you on Cody Patterson. His Dad says he still hasn't heard from him."

Cora nodded and dragged her work gloves off. She rubbed her hands together, feeling the ache of arthritis spreading over her knuckles. "I haven't heard from him either, Bobby. When he dropped off my truck he told me he was going to hoof it back into town. Last I saw of him."

Poole leaned against the wooden fence that corralled Cora's three pigs. He glanced into the muddy pen before speaking. "Just as well, Cora. He was a user that one. I know you thought he was a good kid, but I knew him in school. He had the bite of metal in him."

Cora rested her arms on the railing and sighed. "You never know what's inside a person, Bobby. But eventually they expose their true selves."

The two boars in Cora's pen ignored the people standing over them. They were too interested in their new companion. The black and white one was busy licking her ears, and the white one had mounted her and was furiously humping away.

"You got a new sow," Poole gestured at the fat pink pig that was the object of the others' affections.

Cora nodded.

"I remember Boris and Wilbur. What happened to Duncan? He was huge."

Cora grabbed a stick that had been leaning against the fence and scratched the pink sow's back with it. The pig tried to twitch away from its touch, but its short legs wouldn't let it move far in the mire.

"He went to the butcher's auction in Walnut Valley in July," Cora answered. "Same place she's going to go if she doesn't produce a bunch of little piglets in the spring."

The sow bleated miserably, struggling to get out from under her four-hundred-pound suitor.

Poole removed his hat and ran a hand through his hair. The sun was hot.

"So what's this one's name?"

Cora shrugged. "I just call her Piggy."

GLORIA

Donna L. Greenwood

The odour of the place triggered immediate nausea. I knew that I wouldn't be able to get rid of the smell for hours, despite drenching myself in deodorant. The stench stuck to me like a noxious lover; it reminded me of cabbage and warm piss. It wasn't just the smell that sickened me – walking into the women's high security ward of Belle View Hospital was a multi-sensory vomit-inducing experience. There were metallic clattering sounds, low moans and high shrieks that scratched at your nerves as you walked down each corridor and waited for the nurses to look at your badge and buzz you through. And the air in the place felt thick and treacly, like if you breathed it in, you'd drown in madness. I hated the place, but I was the only available Section 12 approved doctor, so I had no choice but to abandon my lavender-scented, white-washed office and come to this cesspit and assess a new patient – a woman charged with multiple murders. It had been many years since I'd dealt with a serious psychological disorder - I was more used to treating menopausal women with self-esteem problems - so I felt out of my depth as well as sick to the bone.

'Doctor Grayson, hello.' A portly red-faced nurse – the ward sister – was nodding and smiling as she let me through the final door. 'Welcome to Belle View.'

I looked around and was not comforted. After walking through a myriad of locked glass doors, I was finally in the heart of Belle View. The hospital had fifteen beds for women who had been detained under the Mental Health Act – not all were criminals; most were simply in danger of slitting their own throats. It was relatively small compared to most other high-security hospitals and unusual in that it was for women only. The central area was a recreation room with the glassed wall of the nurses' station just to the right. The patients could sit on tiny, doll's house sofas and watch huge televisions that sprawled across the walls above us. To the left was a small dining area that also, so the ward sister told me as she guided me into the nurses' station, doubled up as a visiting room.

'We have five single rooms and five double rooms,' she continued, 'quite luxurious compared to other places. Your patient is in Room 5 at the end of the corridor. It's the only room we keep locked and that's mostly for the safety of the other patients and staff.'

'Well, she's not really my patient; I'm here in place of Doctor Jabeen. I'm doing him a favour. He'll owe me one after this.'

I tried smiling at the nurse but, the truth was, nurses irritated me. Male nurses were fine but female nurses, they seemed to treat female doctors differently to male ones. I felt defensive, almost apologetic, for being a doctor.

'Well, she's your patient for tonight,' said the nurse tersely. She walked over to a large desk overflowing with loose sheets of crumpled paper. She plucked a file from the mess and said:

'You'll find everything you need to know about her in here, but I warn you, Doctor Grayson, she's a tricky one, this one; she's had a couple of my juniors in tears already.'

I looked at the nurse for more information, but she stared back, resolutely not elaborating.

'Okay, give me a few minutes to look over the file and then I'll talk to her. Can I see her some place other than her room? Have you got a private room somewhere?'

'Yes, but I don't think that's advisable. Like I said, she's tricky. There is a police officer on the ward who's supposed to be keeping an eye on her, but she seems more intent on swiping Tinder and smoking fags with the day patients.'

The contempt in her voice was unmistakable. I softened towards her a little; she did seem genuinely harassed.

'You know that I'm here to assess her fitness to plead in court?'

She nodded solemnly.

'Okay, well, anything you can tell me, any observations you've made, can also be used as evidence… so… is there anything you've noticed? Do you think she can stand trial? Do you think she has mental capacity?'

'She's not mad.' The nurse's blunt reply shocked me, especially the use of the word 'mad'. 'She's evil. You know what she did, right? She murdered her friend's children. Three wee souls. The youngest was barely a year old.'

The nurse shook her head. She'd clearly said enough.

She wafted the file in front of my face. 'It's all in here.'

I took the police file from her and sat at her desk without asking permission. The file was thick with notes. The patient's name was Karen Macintosh, she was thirty-two years old and, up until six weeks ago, had had an unblemished record. No sign of any criminal history and no serious medical conditions. I pulled out my tablet from the handbag still slung over my shoulder and tapped into Macintosh's medical records. There was nothing of interest there – she'd had her tonsils taken out when she was eleven, had an ultrasound scan at thirty to find out the cause of heavy periods and was prescribed Omeprazole last year for recurring heartburn. Nothing special. No reports of any psychological problems. That didn't bode well for defence's claim of not guilty by reason of insanity.

I looked again at the file in front of me. Qasim Jabeen had briefed me quickly, over the phone, on the case and had told me that there wasn't sufficient evidence to prove the woman was mentally disordered when she committed the crime – so it was just a case of rubber-stamping her own GP's recommendations and allowing the prosecution to get on with their conviction. I turned over the next page of the report and my stomach heaved. I wasn't expecting photographs, but large snapshots of the crime scene were splayed across the page in front of me. I closed my eyes. Jesus, I was never going to be able to unsee those poor children.

'I told you she was evil. I've never seen anything like it in the twenty-five years I've been working here.' The nurse had been watching me from the corner of the station. I'm pretty sure she wasn't supposed to look through the file, but I had no strength left to argue with her. I took a deep breath and looked again at the pages before me. I tried to concentrate on the words rather than the pictures. Six weeks ago, Karen Macintosh had been at her friend's house drinking wine. According to the file, this was a regular occurrence. Macintosh's friend, Chloe Barnes, had been through a difficult divorce and Macintosh had been her 'rock' through the hard times. According to the report, at about 9.30 pm, Barnes had left the house to get more wine, leaving Macintosh in the house with her three children aged one, three and seven. As I began reading the next paragraph, I once again had to swallow down the urge to vomit. Why the hell had I agreed to this? I knew my strengths – dealing with mid-life crises and phobias – and I knew my weaknesses – dealing with fucking psychos. I'd been a psychiatrist for twenty-seven years. Twelve of those years had been spent studying and training. It was not an easy career to get into. However, after dealing with all manner of misery and madness, after being spat at, shat on, nipped, punched, groped and nipple-twisted, I decided that I no longer wanted to work in the NHS. In truth, I didn't want to deal with mad people, so I set up a private practice and vetted my patients. I only accepted patients who had a healthy bank balance and unhealthy self-esteem. I wasn't ashamed of this decision. I was playing to my strengths and I was very good at what I did.

When Chloe Barnes returned from the shop, she found all three of what remained of her children's bodies placed in a circle. Macintosh was in the centre of the circle covered in blood and eating 'something like steak'. Barnes had screamed and then fainted. The next report was from a neighbour who'd arrived on the scene five minutes later. It was this neighbour who'd removed Barnes from her house and called the police. She described the scene as 'something like *The Texas Chainsaw Massacre*'.

I leafed through the rest of the report, avoiding all pictorial evidence. The coroner's report said that the three children had been beheaded in their sleep. Macintosh had used a butcher's cleaver which had not been in the house previously, suggesting that she had brought the weapon with her and hidden it. Premeditation. I shook my head. She had no chance of an insanity plea. Macintosh had then sliced off the top of the children's dismembered skulls. A spurt of warm vomit shot into my mouth. Good God, what kind of a woman was this? She had arranged the children's bodies into a circle and sat in the centre with their heads on her lap eating the contents of their skulls – their brains. Jesus Christ. Doctor Jabeen had not revealed these little details. He'd just said the woman had killed three children. I'd dealt with murder before. But not this. This was something else.

I swallowed the acidic bile that was collecting in my oesophagus. I'd do this quickly. I just needed to say the woman was sane enough to stand trial and was in control of her actions at the time of the crime. I would be in and out in ten minutes.

'Okay, I'll see her now. I'll see her in her room. Did you say there was a police officer around?'

'Yeah, PC Townson's supposed to be watching her but, like I say, she's not the most fastidious law enforcer I've ever met.'

I walked towards Room 5 with the file under my arm and tablet in my bag. The PC was sitting on a chair outside the room looking at her phone. She barely looked up as I approached her.

'I'm Doctor Grayson – I'm here to speak with Karen Macintosh.'

The police officer stood and put her phone away.

'She's been sleeping for most of the day. Not really much reason for me being here really – that's what the security guards are paid for.'

I think this was an attempt to justify why she'd been on her phone. I nodded as she slid a card key through the lock and opened the door for me.

'Enjoy,' she said and sat back down, retrieving her phone from her jacket pocket.

Macintosh was stretched out, fully clothed, on her bed. She was on her back, with her arms under her head; her eyes were closed and she looked peaceful and most definitely not insane. I coughed, more than a little irritated by her equanimity. I watched as she opened her eyes slowly and yawned. She stretched her arms upwards, did a cat-like stretch of her back, and then turned over on her side, giving me a beaming smile.

'Hello, are you the second opinion?'

I swallowed and pulled up a chair beside her bed.

'I'm Doctor Grayson and I'm here to establish two things, Karen…'

'Miss Macintosh.'

'Sorry?'

'I'd prefer Miss Macintosh. You don't know me.'

'Ok, ahh, Miss Macintosh. I, along with your GP,

Doctor…er…. Ashworth, need to establish whether you were, in some way, mentally diminished, that is, not in control of your actions at the time of the incident and whether or not you are fit to plead in court.'

'I was not in control of my actions, Doctor Grayson. I was possessed by a demon – a *lady* demon.' She looked directly into my eyes. She looked confident, almost cocky, although I did notice she was scratching her left palm rather vigorously.

Here we go, I thought, this is where she tells me some crazy story and tries to persuade me that she's mad. I looked into her eyes. They were clear and bright. They were not the eyes of someone suffering from mental anguish. Convinced that she was playing a game with me, I changed the subject, determined that we were not going to have a conversation about demonic possession. Even if she had some schizophrenic characteristics, it was best not to indulge the fantasies.

'Do you know what year it is, Miss Macintosh?'

I was treated to an exaggerated eye roll and then she sat up, swung her legs over the bed and cocked her head to one side. She continued to scratch at her left palm. I made a brief note of this on my tablet.

'Do you believe that true evil exists, Doctor Grayson?'

'Do you?' – a standard deflection.

'Yes. It's all around us. It haunts the shadows of everything we do. You see…' – she bent forwards, as if she were sharing a secret – 'human beings are essentially pretty good guys. You know, we fall out, we argue, we have our faults, but we're not, you know, evil.'

'Some would argue that humanity is capable of committing deeds that could be called "evil", if we're going to use that word.' The nausea was rising again. I was baiting her, encouraging her, when I should have been assessing her mental capacity and leaving. At no point should we be discussing her alleged crime. We were heading into dangerous waters talking about the nature of evil.

'Nah… human beings are pussies. The worst we would do without the encouragement of demons would be to bash in one another's heads in an argument. No, the truly horrific crimes are committed by those people who have lost control and are instead being controlled by… something else.'

'Demons?' Again, I inwardly admonished myself; this was not relevant.

'What would you call a creature that exists only to take pleasure in the most horrible, most vicious acts of violence? That enjoys watching people die in agonising pain? What would you call someone or something that made you eat the brain of an innocent child?'

Jesus Christ, the bitch was smiling at me. I pulled out the list of assessment questions from my file and asked the second question.

'Do you know who the prime minister of the UK is, Miss Macintosh?'

'You haven't answered my question, Doctor Grayson.' She paused and then said, 'It's 2022. The prime minister is the delightful Boris Johnson – someone who has his own demon problem. I'm not retarded, Doctor Grayson; I don't claim to have a mental disorder. I wish only to state that I was not in control of my actions at the time of the crime. What do you call a creature that makes you eat the brains of a child, Doctor Grayson?'

I didn't like the way she was using my name, over and over. It was irritating me. I looked at my notes for a while and then said:

'I don't believe in what you call "creatures", malevolent or otherwise. Now, tell me about your job, Karen… ah, Miss Macintosh. You worked as a learning mentor at St John's, did you not?'

'I still do. As far as I know, I haven't lost my job. Have I lost my job, Mrs Grayson?'

'It's Doctor Grayson. And, honestly, I don't know. I simply want you to tell me about your work. Did… do you enjoy working with young people?'

'She's here. In this room. We're privileged; she doesn't usually do personal appearances.'

Without thinking, I glanced around the room. It was empty. Through the little glass window in the door, I could see PC Townson swiping her phone.

'There's nobody here except you and I, Miss Macintosh.'

'I can see her. She's standing in the corner of the room staring right at us. I am completely powerless, Doctor Grayson. If Gloria told me to gouge out your eyes, I would have no choice but to comply. She's sitting at the controls, not me.'

'Gloria?'

'Yes, Gloria – my lady demon; she's kind of attached herself to me.'

Despite my better instincts, I pursued this. I was, in some way, still assessing her mental capacity, albeit in a slightly unorthodox way.

'So, Gloria is a demon?'

'I guess so, I mean, I can't think of a better word that

describes something that is so completely and utterly evil.'

'Can Gloria hear us? Can she understand this conversation?'

'She should be able to; she's the one who's doing the talking.'

'Gloria is speaking through you?'

'Kind of. We're sort of synched. Even though she's over there, she's here in my head too. Christ, do you think I'd be this calm if it were just me? I've just eaten my best friend's kids; I'd be slitting my wrists if she wasn't in here with me.'

'Describe Gloria to me.'

'I can't believe you can't see her. She's standing right there. She has to hunch a little because her horns are scraping the ceiling.' Macintosh cocked her head to one side and looked over at the corner of the room. I ignored the urge to look in the same direction.

'She's really big – wide as well as tall – and she's sort of scaly like a dragon but strangely beautiful. Her scales look like black jewels and there're two enormous horns coming out of her head. Her eyes are red as blood…' She stumbled a little here but then seemed to regain her composure. 'She's looking at you.' The scratching of her left palm intensified.

'Karen… Miss Macintosh, I think we both know that there is no one else in this room, that the only two people here are you and I.' I made a note about Macintosh's attempt to make me believe she was hallucinating, then I said, 'Is your hand bothering you?' gesturing towards her frantic scratching.

'That's Gloria's point of entry. She gets into me through my hand. It doesn't hurt; it just itches.'

Macintosh finished her sentence with a vigorous scratch that drew blood. She ignored the blood and continued speaking. 'There is only hell after death, Doctor Grayson. There is no heaven, no promised land. We simply re-live all of our sins, all of our crimes, over and over again.'

I continued to make notes whilst she spoke.

'Do you know that time doesn't really exist? It's a human construct. The human brain has to order its days in a linear, chronological way, otherwise it would go mad. But, actually, everything that ever happened is still happening at some point in the universe. If you travel far enough away from Earth and look back, you would see the Battle of Hastings. If you went back even further, you might catch the moment when Cain bashed in Abel's brains. Do you see what this means?'

I stopped typing and looked up at her. Her left palm was bloody and she was beginning to tear the skin.

'I'm not sure. Perhaps you could explain?'

'It means that every single action we have ever done is still happening at some point in time. If we travelled thousands of light years away from the Earth and looked back with an unfeasibly powerful telescope, you would see me forever munching on Chloe's kids' brains. It means that there are no such things as good and evil. It means that there is no God; there is no divine punishment and there is no salvation. We are damned from the minute we are born.'

'Would you like me to get a nurse to look at that?' I said, pointing to the expanding wound on her left palm. She ignored me and continued:

'No matter what I do, there will be no final reckoning, Doctor Grayson. I have done the worst possible thing I could ever imagine and I'm still here. No bolt of lightning has struck me down. We live in a godless, pitiless universe, Doctor Grayson. I have proven that.'

I smiled.

'I think life is a little more than that, Miss Macintosh. You seem very lucid to me, if a little pessimistic.'

'I'm not saying these words, Gloria is. These are Gloria's thoughts, not mine. How can I be lucid when a monster demon is using me as a puppet?'

I turned off my tablet. I'd heard enough. Even though Macintosh was talking nonsense, she clearly understood her position and what she'd done. I turned away from her and put the tablet back in my bag. I heard the door click open and looked up. PC Townson had just entered the room.

'Doctor Grayson?' she said, looking worried.

'Yes?'

'Who are you talking to?'

I frowned. 'Well, I'm talking to the patient, of course.'

'But she's over there.'

I looked behind me where PC Townson was pointing. There, huddled in the corner, was a cowering woman dressed in a hospital gown. She was shaking and crying. It looked as though she were trying to burrow into the wall behind her.

'But…' I looked back at the bed. It was empty. There was nobody sitting on the bed. I shook my head furiously. What the hell?

'Would you like me to get her into bed for you, Doctor Grayson?'

'No, no, it's fine. Just give me a few more minutes; I'll be finished soon.'

PC Townson nodded but continued to look worried. She left quietly. I waited until I could see her seated in front of the glass pane with her back to me and then I walked over to Karen Macintosh, who was still shaking in the corner. She disgusted me. She reminded me of a scabby dog begging to be kicked. I cocked my head to one side and, with all the force I could muster, I kicked her in the face. Her head flew back and a spray of snotty blood shot from her nose. I walked away. Vermin. That's what humanity is. Vermin. I took a deep breath and pressed the red alarm button. I dropped my bag to the floor so that I could get to my left hand; it was itching like crazy.

MUSICA MORTIS

Wink Taylor

Emmanuel Milton's virtuosity as a pianist was undeniable, and his skills as a composer unquestioned. It was inevitable that he would attend the Royal College of Music in London, and his acceptance into the Royal Philharmonic Orchestra was also of no real surprise. His appearance was as dramatic as his playing. He was over six foot six with black, swept back, flowing hair, an immaculate goatee beard and piercing, dark, flashing eyes. He looked like the very personification of a brooding Tocata by Bach. He strutted the concert halls of Europe with overweening self-confidence and a discordant streak of arrogance. Before too long, there was less talk of the prodigious talent and more discussion of the 'character problem'. With all the epic certainty of an Italian opera, Milton was slowly replaced by less competent composer/musicians who were much easier to work with. Railing against this, only exacerbated the situation, and as the work offers dried up, Milton retreated into teaching, occasional music notation work, self-pity and fearsome bitterness.

He lived in a three-storeyed terraced mews in a once fashionable area of Chelsea. He had a number of students, but none were particularly exceptional. Their parents were won over by Milton's impressive credentials and were more than happy to pay his exorbitant fees. Despite their children's lack of progress and Milton's utter disdain, the parents never once dared question the Maestro's teaching.

Once the intrusion of having to spend time with his students was over, Milton would launch himself at the piano, furiously striking the keys. Chord structure after chord structure would be thrown to inspiration in the hope that one would flower into a melody, but always the seed would fail to take root and all Milton's attempts at creativity would just descend into angry collapse.

'I must find it,' Milton sighed, refusing to commit to failure, but surrendering to self-imposed melancholia. 'I must find the piece that will bring me back!'

Sometimes he would encounter a moment. A refrain that would stir his soul. It was as if a door had opened to reveal treasures within. But as hard as he tried, he found he could never capture and develop the moment; the inspiration drained away like sand between his fingers. These were the days of Emmanuel Milton. Uninspiring teaching, uninspiring composing, uninspiring life.

Then … he heard a knock on the door.

'Good evening. I saw your advertisement within *The Times*. I understand that you notate music.'

The man that stood in Milton's doorway was tall and thin. His sensitive face revealed a vulnerability that, at first, Milton took for weakness, but the piercing blue eyes hinted at a core of steel beneath.

'My name is Peter Fielding,' the man said removing his hat in an oleaginous manner that Milton found vaguely disgusting. However, the ensuing handshake was firm and strong. Milton couldn't decide if Fielding was as light as a waltz or as deep as a symphony.

'How can I help you, Mr Fielding?' Milton enquired.

'I have a composition,' Fielding said diffidently. 'I have never learnt to write music, I'm afraid. I can only play. I would be grateful if you could … transcribe my playing into a piece of manuscript I could take away.'

Milton noted, with disgust, Fielding's difficulty in pronouncing the letter r in the word 'transcribing'. Such degeneracy offended Milton's desire for perfection, and it was all he could do to resist slamming the door in Fielding's face.

'I'm sorry, Mr Fielding, but I am a very busy man,' Milton said, gradually closing the door.

Fielding blocked him, stepping forward with a firmness that made Milton gasp.

'Mr Milton, please?' Fielding implored.

Finding himself unable to close the door, Milton glanced down and saw that Fielding had jammed his foot in the door.

'Mr Fielding, I am unable to help you with this matter and I wish you a good night!' Milton snarled, belying the politeness of the wish.

But Fielding was nothing if not persistent. 'Mr Milton, I have researched your work meticulously and believe you are the only musician sensitive enough to transcribe this work. I need your passion… You are my only hope.' He clawed at Milton's arm, pulling on the plush velvet of his smoking jacket in desperation.

'If you do not unhand me, Mr Fielding, I will be forced to call the police.'

'One thousand pounds!' Fielding shouted, his face

shining with perspiration. 'Just hear me play the piece, give me your honest opinion as a musician, and I'll give you the money there and then. And if you do not wish to continue any further, then you will never hear from me again.' Fielding then slumped in resignation. If Milton refused even this offer, he had no cards left to play.

With all pressure on the door released, Milton once more was in control. The thousand pounds would mean he could turn down some of his students and have more time for composition.

'Well, Mr Fielding, it would appear to be an interesting proposition,' Milton purred. Then not wanting to be seen as avaricious, he quickly introduced the subject of music. 'However, I must warn you, as a serious musicologist I will spare no quarter in the honesty of my critique.'

'That is what I want,' Fielding said quietly.

'And the one thousand pounds?' Milton asked with an uncomfortable smile.

'It is here,' Fielding said, reaching into the inside pocket of his overcoat.

Fearing the tittle-tattle and gossip of his neighbours that might follow him being sighted on his own doorstep conducting a cash transaction, Milton beckoned the stranger inside. 'Come in, Mr Fielding. A gentleman should never discuss money in public.'

'In my experience, gentlemen in public rarely discuss anything else,' said Fielding, transfixing Milton with an ice-blue stare.

Milton smiled through a grimace; Fielding had once more shown a flash of something dark within. Milton felt unnerved. 'Allow me to take your hat and coat, Mr

Fielding?' he said, determined to regain control by assuming the role of perfect host.

'Thank you,' Fielding said, surveying his new surroundings. 'What a beautiful house.'

'Thank you. The piano is in the drawing room. Would you kindly step this way?'

'I assume you bought this place whilst you were with the Royal Philharmonic?'

'Yes, that's quite right,' Milton said, mildly surprised by the depth of Fielding's knowledge of his past.

'Before the Arts Council forced you out, saying that they would withdraw funding if you continued to be employed. Something to do with various temper-related misdemeanours? Is that right?'

Milton felt his blood begin to boil at such impertinence. 'If you've come here to insult me, Mr Fielding, I can assure you that no amount of money will—'

'I am merely stating the facts. Now, shall we go over to the piano?' Fielding spoke quietly, but accompanied his words with a stare so icy that it might freeze an inferno.

'Follow me!' Milton snapped. He opened the double doors to the drawing room. Spying a set of golden pokers by the fireplace, Milton suppressed the desire to wipe the smirk off Fielding's face by taking the implements and caving in his skull. He imagined the sound of Fielding's head cracking open like an egg. With a smile, he then allowed himself to speculate on what musical key would match that sound.

Fielding sat at the piano. He lifted the lid and surveyed the eighty-eight keys before him, and then he slowly turned to face Milton, revealing the tears that streamed down his face. The eyes which had previously hinted at a steely determination now seemed to cry out a depth of melancholy beyond Milton's experience.

'I have not told you of my late wife, Mr Milton. She was an incredible woman, who had the greatest belief in me. I owe her everything, Mr Milton. Without her I am nothing!'

The power of the emotion Fielding was displaying rendered Milton dumbstruck and he felt frighteningly out of his depth. This was a feeling alien to a man who prided himself on his self-control. He hated the sensation and the man who had caused it.

'So, I have composed this piece as a tribute to my wife,' Fielding continued. 'A Requiem. Music for her memory. Shall I play it for you now?' he asked weakly.

Milton nodded, but really wanted to slam the piano lid down on Fielding's long sensitive fingers and see the skin break. To see the blood come to the surface and perhaps catch a glimpse of white bone protruding through the fleshy pulp.

'I shall begin,' Fielding stated. He slowly sat upright, breathed in and allowed his fingers to descend upon the keys.

What followed was a sound Milton had never heard before. On paper, the music would have looked ludicrously simple. The piece consisted of a simple descent pattern of chords within a minor key, and to any musician of even middling quality it would have been trivial to play. However, despite this, the combination of the simplicity of the music, the passion of the playing and the sheer visceral nature of the piece was overwhelming.

As the piece continued, Milton found himself grasping for a sense of balance. He forced himself to sit down before he fell down, never once taking his eyes off the concentrated form at the piano, never once allowing himself to be distracted from the music. And oh, what music! A music like no other. A music that spoke of the depths within and without. A music that seemed to be the very essence of life. A music that felt like it was the very breath of God.

When Fielding had finished playing, he sat at the piano like a man who had emptied his very soul. It was as if the very act of playing had aged him. His skin was manuscript-paper white but parchment thin. He inhaled sharply, as if doing so was like a final act of resuscitation.

'What do you think of the composition, Mr Milton?'

Milton sat aghast, his eyes filled with tears. In a broken voice he simply replied, 'It was miraculous!'

'Then you will agree to the work?'

Milton was still reeling from the effect the music had engendered and was too distracted to continue with the act of the great composer. In the wake of this musical epiphany, he was truly humbled.

'It will be my honour, Mr Fielding.'

Fielding smiled and stood up. The broken wraith-like figure from before was disappearing and Fielding's strength was returning. 'I shall return tomorrow evening and the work will begin.' His tone was brisk and business-like. 'I welcome, of course, any suggestion from you as to how the music can be improved upon, but any alterations must be true to the memory of Helen. That, I must insist upon. Do I make myself clear?'

'Yes, of course,' Milton stammered. He felt uncertain

and anxious. The music had sparked such a creative reawakening, his brain was dancing with inspiration; however, Fielding's manner now threatened to nullify the spark.

'Mr Fielding, perhaps we could start tonight?' Milton implored, anxious to gorge at the musical feast once more.

'No! I am too tired,' Fielding sighed.

Milton once again felt a wave of disgust for the man. How could Fielding be so determined one minute and so weak the next? And how could he deny him, Milton, the sound of the extraordinary music again.

'I shall return tomorrow. Shall we say eight o'clock?'

'Yes, eight o'clock, or sooner if you wish.'

The two men walked through the hall to the door. Fielding put on his hat and coat.

'Oh, by the way. Your fee.' Fielding handed over the one thousand pounds. 'For services rendered,' he added with a slight caustic smile.

Milton took the money with all the joy of a condemned man. As Fielding's sapphire eyes held him in a penetrating gaze, Milton felt grubby and underhand. He disliked intensely the term 'for services rendered'. It was as if he had been involved in a transaction of seediness, as if his life-fought skills were being likened to those of a whore plying her trade.

'Until tomorrow, Mr Fielding.'

Fielding made no reply and Milton watched him leave.

Then, when alone Milton writhed like a worm on a pin. He felt such hatred that it threatened to consume him. Fielding had a sure and steady way of making Milton feel diminished, like a wrong note in the middle of a recital. Once again, he began to have thoughts of violence. But his desire for brutality was constantly countered by thoughts of the music – music that kept floating upon his memory and imagination. An inescapable melody that touched the heart and burned through to the core. It was the music of the Gods. Anyone who could compose music like that had to be a messenger from the Heavens. Why did it have to be Fielding? Why couldn't it be he, himself?

* * *

'The C-sharp within the G chord does not work. It is discordant.'

'Precisely the effect I want, Mr Milton.'

'But musically it does not work,' Milton said emphatically.

'Mr Milton, I greatly appreciate some of the suggestions you have made. You have made some significant improvements to the piece, but this is non-negotiable. For, you see, this piece must reflect Helen herself.'

'I say again, Fielding, it is discordant!' Milton snapped, hurling his pencil to the floor and theatrically flouncing to a chair at the other end of the drawing room.

'But Helen was discordant!' Fielding cried. He then paused for breath, before continuing in a calmer tone, some moments later. 'Helen was the most discordant person I have ever met.' A smile crossed his face; he was suddenly lost in a nostalgia. 'She couldn't fit in if she tried.'

Milton exhaled … loudly. He shuffled uncomfortably in his chair at the thought of being treated to yet another story about the wonderful Helen. This had been the pattern of the entire evening, fond reminiscence rather than serious music. He looked at the paper knife on his desk and relished the thought of plunging it deep into Fielding's chest. He smiled at the thought of the blood spouting from Fielding's thin frame, all set, in his mind, to the bombastic strains of the 1812 Overture. The mental image of Fielding gagging on his own blood, choking to Tchaikovsky, amused him.

'I would say to Helen, "But Darling, you must try and mix with people a bit more," and she would reply, "What's the point, dear? So long as we have each other, who cares?" We would laugh for hours about that. Dear, dear Helen.' Fielding was totally lost in his memories; a beatific smile stretched across his gaunt face.

Resisting the temptation to tell Fielding that his wife sounded perfectly horrid, Milton stood up briskly. 'Come on, Fielding, let's return to the composition.'

'Yes, we must. But you see now, Mr Milton, this music must reflect Helen absolutely. When I hear this music I want to see all of her. You do understand, don't you? This music must bring her back to me. You see, this music is all I've got!'

Milton turned away, hiding his look of disgust at Fielding's cascading tears.

'I apologise, Mr Milton. Now, we were discussing the C-sharp?' Fielding asked falteringly.

Milton faced him again, anxious to return to the subject of music – the subject he had dedicated his life to with such ruthlessness. The subject that had made him the master. Why was it he now felt like an amateur? Fielding's complete lack of regard for musical convention had created a masterpiece. A masterpiece that Milton knew he could never create.

'I believe we had agreed upon the addition of the C-sharp,' Milton said bitterly. 'Shall we now move on?'

* * *

As the days went by, Fielding became an obsession that began to haunt Milton's every waking hour. Milton was ashamed to admit that he found himself living for his sessions with Fielding. He wanted to know more about the man and to find the answer to the question that burned Milton's soul: how could Fielding create such music?

Milton had made enquiries into Fielding's background, but had found not even the slightest hint of musical profundity. Fielding had been an unremarkable student and by all accounts a mediocre draughtsman by trade. He had walked through life without causing the merest ripple.

One afternoon, Milton elected to follow Fielding. After a slow meandering walk, Milton saw Fielding enter a graveyard. Hiding behind a headstone, Milton watched as Fielding stood at a well-tended grave.

'Hello Helen, my darling,' Fielding said gently.

Milton grimaced at such sentiment, disgusted that Fielding was conducting a conversation with a grave.

'It's almost finished, my darling. It's sounding wonderful. It so reminds me of you. It's everything I could have wanted and more. Mr Milton has been most helpful.'

Milton's ears pricked up at the sound of his name.

'You were so right about him, my dear. He is a

marvellous composer. Do you remember when we saw him play at St Martins-in-the-Field? He was so passionate. Well, he has helped me so much and I think it will be finished tonight. Goodbye, my dear.'

Milton watched in revulsion as Fielding kissed the headstone and slowly wandered away. Once Fielding was out of sight, Milton emerged from his hiding place and walked over to Mrs Fielding's grave. He examined the monolithic, grey headstone and read the words carved deep within the limestone: 'Here lies Helen Fielding, beloved wife of Peter.' Milton then saw at the base of the tombstone some extra words. He inexplicably felt a shudder; his blood ran cold and his scalp began to prickle. He felt as if he were intruding upon something that was best left alone. He read the words: 'Death is but a door.'

∗ ∗ ∗

'Have you notated the descent into the D minor chord, Mr Milton?' Fielding asked.

'Naturally!' Milton snapped, scrawling furiously on the manuscript paper.

'May I see it?' Fielding enquired irritably.

'When I have finished transcribing,' Milton carped.

Both men were exhausted. They had started at six o'clock and had not stopped for almost six hours. As Milton handed over the manuscript, Fielding snatched at the paper as if it were a lifeline. He perused the manuscript with fearsome attentiveness. Milton saw the veins on Fielding's forehead throb in sheer concentration.

'Well?' Milton interrogated.

Fielding wiped a bead of perspiration from his brow

and smiled in relief. 'It is finished! Oh good heavens … it is finished!'

Fielding slumped in his seat and looked like a man who had just won a reprieve. Milton ran over to him and shook his hand.

'Well done, Fielding. Well done!'

'I couldn't have done it without you. Thank you, thank you,' Fielding grinned.

Milton's immediate instinct was one of euphoria, a delight in a difficult job being completed successfully, but now he began to feel differently. His work with Fielding had given him joy and a sense of fulfilment. It had filled a vacuum in his life … and he would miss it.

'Are you sure it is complete?' Milton asked weakly, 'I feel we may have missed something.'

'No, no, no – it is perfect as it is.'

'I may have made a mistake.'

'What you? I think we know, my friend, that when it comes to notating music, you never make mistakes.'

Was Fielding teasing him again? Milton resisted the desire to rise to the slight, the composition was too important. As Fielding began putting the manuscript papers into his briefcase, Milton felt like an old friend was being snatched away from him.

'When the piece is finally performed, Fielding, will you allow me to play it?'

'I beg your pardon, dear boy?' Fielding asked in surprise.

'I presume that is your plan. A piece of such importance is made to be heard. Where do you plan on performing it?' Milton asked, in a tone bordering on hysteria.

Fielding stopped dead and stared at his overwrought companion. 'It shall never be played. This piece is for Helen,' he stated incredulously.

'Come come, Mr Fielding, we all know that this piece is revolutionary. If you were to premiere this around the concert halls, you would not only cause consternation but also make a small fortune. And furthermore you—'

'Mr Milton!' Fielding shouted. His blue eyes were ablaze with a mix of fear and anger. 'Have you understood nothing during our time together? This is a tribute to my late wife!'

Milton rushed over to Fielding, grabbing his arm as he did so. 'Your late wife, Mr Fielding. She's dead and will never hear this work!' he snarled, tightening his grip.

'Release me at once. You're hurting me!' Fielding pushed Milton away, who was breathing very heavily.

'My wife was not a social woman, Milton. I have told you this before. People were not her first priority. They didn't have to be – we had each other. When I play this music, it will be as if she is in the room with me once more. Why would I want to share her with other people? I thank you for your work and I will now take my leave of you.' Fielding finished putting the papers into his briefcase and then reached for his hat and coat.

Milton stared at Fielding utterly disconsolate. The greatest piece of music he had ever worked upon was about to walk out of his life forever. Memories of past failures crashed jaggedly into his mind, each one causing pain. Memories of the dismissals, the barbed comments, the opportunities missed, the relationships betrayed, the struggles both physical and mental. The chance to wipe these away was about to disappear from his life in the form of a frail, lovesick, sentimental fool selfishly clutching Milton's life's work.

Looking down at his hands, Milton saw them flex and twist into claws. They suddenly looked huge and engorged. He imagined them wrapped around Fielding's scrawny, thin neck squeezing and crushing. Then, in reality, he felt the man's life in his hands gradually ebbing away, the twitching body in a feeble battle for survival it could not win. A red mist of rage had enveloped Milton like a straitjacket. His actions were no longer his own, but he was aware of every single nerve-shredding moment.

Milton only regained complete control when Fielding's body slumped to the floor. He picked up the poker from the ornamental stand and stood over the crawling, rasping body that was fighting for breath.

'And now for the coda, Mr Fielding.'

The noise of solid brass against skull was more satisfying than Milton imagined it would be, and he became quite disappointed when the blows fell against more floor than bone. He noted with amusement … the key was A-flat.

* * *

As the garden was surrounded by a high brick wall, there was no fear of being seen. Fielding's slight frame was not difficult to lift and even easier to conceal in a small plot of earth behind the hydrangeas. The work was speedily executed as Milton was impatient to return to the piano — to return to the music that would resurrect his career indefinitely. He would telephone the conductors of all the major orchestras and invite them around in the morning.

He would announce to the world of music that he was back – back with a composition that would put him in the highest echelons of the musical firmament.

Once his arrangements had been concluded, he lifted the lid of the piano. The keys stared at him like teeth within a skull. Milton pondered with a smile, all he needed to do to change his life forever was to press the keys in sequential order with varying degrees of pressure, to cause the small hammers to strike the strings which would ring out the tune. What a miraculous machine! A true box of delights. As Milton stared at the piano, he felt illuminated. It was as if this moment were everything he had ever lived for. It was as if he were now in the presence of God. He sat on the plush velvet upholstery of the piano stool and breathed deeply. The sheet music was in place, his posture assumed; this was now his moment.

As soon as his hands touched the keyboard, it was as if they were no longer his own. The music flowed from him. The piano had never sounded so good. The bass was rich and deep, the treble light and delicate like water drops. The music filled the air and permeated its way through every dimension of the room. Milton felt tears fall from his eyes in cascades. The music was profound and full. The emotions the music evoked were pulled from his soul. It was overwhelming. It was consuming him, drowning him.

Milton tried to pull his hands away, but the playing continued. His fingers danced across the keys, stretching for notes that were never available to him in the past. The music suddenly rose in ferocity, as if building to an earth-shattering crescendo which never came. It was intensity followed by yet more intensity. Milton was trapped on a carousel of music with no end. As the sweat poured from his face, he let out a fearsome scream. His perfect pitch meant that it fitted brilliantly within the music.

Milton felt on the verge of collapse, his head lolled from side to side, but still the music went on. He could hear the wind and rain outside, lashing at his window. An occasional crackle of lightning and a rumble of thunder added a percussive beat to the symphony around him. The moments of heart-rending simplicity within the tune would bring images crashing into Milton's mind. Snapshots of his failures, his wrath, an image of a hand emerging from a grave. He writhed in pain at the thought of Fielding, murdered by his own hand. The sight of those pain-filled blue eyes staring up at him. The images constantly replayed again and again in his mind, all accompanied by the music. A Mass. A Mass of death.

He then suddenly and dreadfully became aware of a relentless pulse that underscored the composition. At first, Milton thought it was his own heartbeat; then he realised its true nature. It was the sound of footfall. Someone or something was walking down the hallway. Milton wanted to run in fear, but he was held in place at the piano. The music was no longer salvation; it was now his captor.

A new sound was now added to the cacophony. The sound of stertorous breathing on top of the approaching footsteps. Now the footfall was closer, the volume grew and Milton could hear that one foot was being dragged. The breathing contained a rattling sound and a rasp. He could also hear something new. It was the sound of earth hitting the hallway's parquet flooring.

Milton's advanced sensitivity of hearing was always

something he had prided himself on, never realising it would one day be a curse. For at that moment, he also heard something else – a slow perverse giggle. Perhaps it was the giggle of a child or the laughter of the truly mad. His hearing also revealed something else, a new sound. The sound of a sob and a scream. To his horror, he realised that this sound was his own.

The drawing room's double doors were thrown open and Milton screamed at the sight that stood before him. The emaciated figure limped forward. The stench made Milton retch. Hanging from the spectre were dangling tendrils of flesh that seemed to dance to the rhythm of the music. The eyeless sockets held Milton transfixed, as a skeletal claw slowly advanced in the direction of his throat. As the ghastly, rotting figure of Helen Fielding leaned over him, Milton saw in his peripheral vision another form step into the room. It was the blood and earth–stained figure of Peter Fielding. His blue eyes flashed, contrasting neatly with the crimson blood that gushed from his open skull. Fielding stared at Milton. His eyes held a combination of accusation and triumph. There was also something else … could it be gratitude?

As the stick like fingers gradually squeezed his throat, Milton stared at Fielding and smiled. Now, he understood. Music had dominated and ruled Milton's life; whilst for Fielding, music was life. Fielding had been right all along. The music had brought Helen back to him. As life fell away, Milton saw the Fieldings together again. Reunited in death forever.

It was probably the nicest thought Milton had ever had.

THE DOORMAN

Justin Cawthorne

Night.

The quiet death. The time for all things to go away. Except—

A sound rang ugly-happy in the darkness, calling him back into the light. Sean crept away, trying to stay hidden.

Ding-ding dong!

It came again, waking him up this time. The front doorbell. Someone at the door! Someone in the night. Sean lay still, waiting for the world to catch up with him—or was it the other way around?

His heart pounded. His head raced through the hundred or so reasons why his doorbell shouldn't be ringing at this hour, and the one or two that could possibly explain why it was. The urge to stay in bed, to draw the covers over himself and ignore the sound, was immense.

Ding-ding dong!

Again.

Whoever it was, they weren't about to let him sleep. No one rang a doorbell at night unless it was important— unless it was something that couldn't possibly wait until morning.

Sean got out of bed and reached for his dressing gown.

Before he could persuade himself to do otherwise, he was marching down the hallway towards the front door. *Get it over with quick.* He didn't *want* to know what was waiting for him on the other side, he didn't *want* to deal with whoever it was, but there was no choice. Maybe a fire in the neighbourhood? The police? Could someone have died? He ran through the list of choices—any close friends or relatives whose unexpected deaths might require his immediate attention—and came up depressingly short.

He reached the door, unlocked it with still-sleeping, fumbling hands, and pulled it open, just an inch or two.

'This'd better be important,' he said, his voice still not quite awake. 'Do you know what time it—'

He stopped. There was no one there: just cold, empty night air. He was talking to himself.

Sean shook his head. Perhaps he had dreamt it. Much better. Yes, that made sense. He locked the door and returned to bed.

* * *

Ding-ding dong!

Sean sat up, eyes wide.

Ding-ding dong!

Definitely real. Not dreaming. He looked at the clock, wondering how long it had been. But he hadn't thought to check it the first time. Must have fallen back to sleep.

Blood hammered inside his head. His heart thumped. It was so dark. Everything around him was black and alien, shadows smothering the familiarity out of his home.

The intrusion of the doorbell had pulled him into a world he normally hid from.

He took a few deep breaths, slowing himself down. Then he once again wrapped himself in his dressing gown and walked to the door. His mind busily reminded himself of all the bad things that might be waiting for him when he got there. He ignored it all and opened the door.

No one there.

Nothing.

The doorstep was empty.

A prank…? But the night was free of the tell-tale sounds of giggling, or of footsteps running away. Nothing lurked beneath the gentle murmur of the darkness.

Hiding? Sean stepped out of his house. His nerves were a tripwire; he was ready to either retreat or lash out, depending on what was waiting for him. The shadows lying past the edge of his doorway slowly cleared, revealing nothing along the front of his house.

But there are so many places to hide …

He stepped further out, sufficiently emboldened to take a proper look around.

The driveway. The bins. The hedge. All clear. No one there.

He continued into the street. Empty.

Must have been kids. Bored kids with nowhere else to go; just happened to pick his house for their pranks. With any luck they'd have tired of him already and moved on to their next victim. Sean headed back into his house, the relief that there was no one to deal with far greater than any anger that had started to build inside.

* * *

Sean stopped to take a final look outside before closing his front door. The latch slid home again with a reassuring click. He turned away.

Ding-ding dong!

He froze. How could someone have gotten to the bell so fast? They would have had to have been standing next to him as he walked back into the house. But there had been no one. He had *looked*.

His legs trembled, threatening to falter beneath him. His skin prickled as the fear and confusion grew. He didn't understand what was happening, except that someone was doing it to *him*. Someone was out there, but he couldn't see them. Why him? Why him???

Ding-ding dong!

Ding-ding dong ding-ding dong ding-ding dong ding-ding dong!

Sean clasped his hands over his ears, trying to banish the sound. He wanted nothing more than to curl up in the corner of the hallway and hide. The button for the doorbell was right there, next to the door where it always was, but he knew if he opened the door right that second and looked outside he would see that *no one was there*. How could they—

Then he understood.

The doorbell was wireless. The button broadcast its summons to a speaker in the kitchen. Maybe the battery was running low, or something was interfering with the signal. Either way, all he needed to do was unplug the speaker—shut it up for the night—and head back to bed.

He double-checked that the front door was locked and went into the kitchen.

* * *

Sean stood and stared at the empty socket: the one where the speaker for the doorbell was supposed to sit. It was nearly a minute before the breath that had locked up in his chest finally forced its way out.

The speaker wasn't there.

Had he moved it?

But … when…?

He tried to remember, even though he knew he hadn't touched it. That could only mean …

… someone else had moved it.

A wave of fear sharp enough to make him dizzy passed over. He reached for the kitchen counter, grabbing the edge to steady himself.

And saw the small, black mobile phone sitting there.

It wasn't his.

Someone had been in his house.

He reached for the phone, thinking he would just take it to the front door and throw it out of his house—*get rid of the damn thing*—and almost dropped it when it rang in his hand.

Ding-ding dong!

It had been programmed to make the same sound as his doorbell. That's what he had been hearing. That was how they could ring the doorbell without being at the door.

But where were—

Sean's fear spiralled as he stared at the phone's screen: at the number that was calling.

It was his number.

His home phone number.

They were using his phone!

He leaned across the counter, peering into the front

room, to the coffee table where the phone normally sat.

The cradle was empty.

They had his phone.

They were inside the house—

Ding-ding dong!

Sean jerked back in fright, hitting his head on the wall behind. His vision blurred. Distantly, he saw the mobile phone fall from his hand to the tiled floor with a plastic crack. But it still kept ringing.

He backed away from it, looking wildly into every shadow. *Where were they hiding???* The spare bedroom? The hallway? Somewhere around the corner, just out of sight?

He forced his legs to move. There was no choice. Someone was in the house; he needed to get out. He made it out of the kitchen, somehow keeping the panic from overwhelming him. His nerves were ready to shatter.

Keep going. Steady steps. *Hurry.* Not far from the door now. Once he made it to the street he could run and never stop. He wouldn't be trapped anymore.

Behind him, something *crunched* in the kitchen

They were coming after him!

The panic took over. Sean ran. He saw his front door. Too far away. Someone was right behind him. His bedroom was closer. Right there.

Go!

He ran inside and slammed the door shut with both arms. With his eyes never leaving the door, he stepped away, retreating towards the bed. The door was surely about to open any second. Whoever it was would come marching in after him. He felt the wall against his back and pressed himself into it, getting as far from the door as he could, eyes never leaving the handle.

Then he heard it.

Footsteps.

It was really happening. Someone in his house. His thoughts tornadoed. His heart tried to beat free of his chest. His head swam, the fear carrying it somewhere apart from the rest of him. There was nothing he could do. Just … *stop!*

Step.

Step.

Step …

The footsteps came. Unhurried. Deliberate. Closer. Closer. Moving up the hallway. Coming for him. Up to his door. Right outside.

Then stopped.

Sean waited for the sound of the door handle turning. He couldn't focus. His head kept trying to pull him somewhere dark and spinning and far away. But he needed to stay in this room. The door pushed and pulled away from him, pulsating in the dark, shadows falling deeper and deeper across it. The rushing in his ears drowned out everything.

In the darkness the door waited ahead of him, growing smaller and smaller at the end of the tunnel. The footsteps continued in the distance. Somewhere, another door finally opened.

Then silence.

Then blackness.

∗ ∗ ∗

Sean woke up, unsure how long he had been on the floor. His legs were numb. His back ached, contorted between the wall and bedside cabinet.

It was still dark.

He listened.

Silence.

Whoever had been in the house was gone. He couldn't explain how he knew; only that his home felt … *his* once again.

He got up and hobbled towards the bedroom door, ignoring the brief fear that there would be someone standing right outside waiting for him.

He opened it. There was no one there.

It was cold in the hallway. Unusually cold.

The front door had been left wide open.

An icy knot of fear gripped Sean's chest. He had almost fooled himself into believing that he had imagined it all. But here was proof.

Someone had been there: inside his home.

He walked over to close the door, ready to run at every step, expecting someone to step from the shadows, expecting to see the monstrous bulk of them framed in the empty doorway.

Then he saw the note.

It sat on the small table by the door, crinkling in the night breeze, held in place by one of the smooth white stones from his front garden.

He stared at it mutely, desperately wanting to not touch it. Whatever the piece of paper was, it wasn't his. It couldn't be. Someone had left it there: someone who had been in his house. It was for them; not for him.

He reached out for the front door, stretching his arm

as far as it would go, desperate to close the door before someone could jump out and grab him from the other side. The door teetered on its hinges, buffeted by the breeze, then swung mercifully shut. Sean rushed forward to lock it and collapsed on the doormat, sweating with relief.

His eyes went to the table, drawn to the note that still sat there demanding his attention. He could just leave it if he wanted to. Ignore it. He didn't need to look at it.

But …

He reached over, pushed the stone away, and picked up the note. He was safe now. It was all over. A mere note couldn't hurt him.

He stared at what had been written for him, and felt the fear crushing him again. The page had been ripped from one of his own notebooks. On it was a handwritten message.

Just three words:

See you tomorrow …

BELLE

The Secret Submissive

*H*ow *many strangers do you encounter on a daily basis? We probably see tens to hundreds of faces every day – each with its own story to share, worries to hide and sins to disguise. We travel through life making snap judgements about the person behind that passing face all the time – the lady on the bus, the boy that serves our burrito – but with less than a minute's thought; they enter and exit our minds and are lost forever.*

Every once in a while, however, those passing faces spark a curiosity that we yearn to explore – like an itch that needs to be scratched – and so, we make small talk and we ask questions; we narrow the distant gap between two foreign faces, even if only for a short while.

Bars and clubs are undeniably one of the places where the gap is at its narrowest. Under the partial disguise of darkness, and injected with alcohol-fuelled confidence, strangers become friends and friends become lovers, all in a matter of hours. One-night stands are considered a rite of passage for so many people and a delicious form of escapism for so many others, but how well do we really know anybody? What secrets are lurking behind that polished exterior? Do we ask the questions that we need to when our primal desires take hold of rationality?

Maybe, just maybe, next time you see a face that ignites your interest, you should stop and think twice... what enigmas reside behind those enticing eyes?

The suit helps, it's true, but in the end, they always see what they want to see – the truth doesn't matter. Jack slipped off his wedding band and tucked it into the inside pocket of his jacket. He tried to massage away the smooth indentation, but twenty-six years of marriage was bound to leave its mark. He buried the thought and allowed himself to revel in the moment instead – to enjoy the twinge of anticipation knotting in the pit of his stomach. He didn't need to think about his wife tonight.

With its sticky floor and watered-down whisky, Luna Bar was a far cry from his usual Friday night haunts of cocktail lounges and rooftop bars; but there was something comforting about the smell of cheap cigarettes outside and uncut desperation inside. It brought him back, even though the risk of exposure grew more and more substantial with every visit. He desperately needed to hunt tonight – it had been far too long. He craved warm meat and this place was crawling with supple, young flesh. It was a slaughterhouse of doe-eyed, scantily clad, young lambs, all ready and willing to play his game, to satisfy his every desire.

As he swirled his whisky with a steady, calculated rhythm, he caught sight of his reflection in the locked screen of his phone. His eyes were gaunt, hollow almost; streaks of grey dominated his once thick, chestnut-brown hair. *Just a semblance of everything you used to be*, the spectral figure whispered back at him, taunting him in muted tones. His fingers trembled – wet from the condensation sliding down the outer edge of the chipped glass. Knocking back the remainder of his drink in one assured mouthful, he drowned the doubts, choked out the weakness and centred his focus on the task at hand.

That was when he saw her.

She looked completely out of place amongst the throng of borderline alcoholics, idlers and cheap tarts. Propped on a pedestal at the opposite side of the bar, she sipped on a deep red elixir through a candy-striped straw, careful not to smudge her perfectly applied, pillar-box red lipstick. Her nails were perfectly manicured too, in the same shade of red as her lipstick. He drank in her beauty, from her delicate ankles to her milky, exposed thighs and upwards. He throbbed unwittingly as she leaned forward and presented her pert breasts for his viewing pleasure. Her slender body was concealed by only the thinnest of fabrics, which wrapped around her in the form of a skin-tight, little, black dress. She was classically beautiful, and in the dim light of the bar, she looked barely twenty years old. *This is too easy*, Jack smirked to himself, arrogance displacing all reservations.

A rumour of a breeze caressed the nape of her neck and goosebumps arose on her arms; she sensed his presence before she saw him. 'Another drink for the lady?' He exuded charm and charisma that only an older man could possess. A flicker of hope kindled in the very depths of her core. He repositioned the bar stool which stood beside her. Taking it back, a foot or so, he used the distance to lull her into a sense of comfortability.

'I'm okay, thanks,' she smiled coyly, tucking a thick length of her dark hair behind her ear. She tried to contain the flicker as his smile caused her to spark and ignite. And how *he* longed to wrap her lustrous waves around his fist. She smelled as sweet as she looked, he noted. His presence must have put her at ease immediately because she didn't retreat, as she had done with the others. He was a gentleman, after all – or maybe it was just the suit? Either way, she invited his proximity. 'I think I'm in the wrong place, to be honest – I told the driver to take me to Luna Sphere. I'm supposed to be meeting my friends, so I ought to be going.' Her eyes seemed to penetrate him as if he were a puzzle that she was desperate to solve. She examined the creases on his forehead, the small angular scar on his jaw, looking for any clue – any traces of who, why, what, when or where.

Luna Sphere was in the city centre. *So, she's alone and a good thirty minutes from where she should be – excellent*, Jack reflected, recalculating his angle of approach. He steeled his doubts and buried any concerns of propriety. *God, she smells delicious…* he needed a taste; he needed to devour her.

'Well, I'm happy to keep you company. I wouldn't want my little girl out alone in a place like this at night. I'm Jack, by the way.' Her eyes brightened at hearing his words – the air of fruitlessness that had eclipsed the evening suddenly dissipated.

Maybe this could be the night? she hoped and prayed. She swivelled towards him, letting her stiletto heel rest against his leg. She looked across at his body, gauging his reaction as she reached out to him.

'I'm Annabel, but you should call me Belle – like in *Beauty and the Beast*.' The sultry darkness behind her mascaraed eyes captivated and connected with the depravity of Jack's desires. She was awakening the beast within – teasing and provoking him with her pouting lips and the tender tone of her voice. He shuffled uncomfortably as the innocence that lined her words tugged him firmly to attention. Would she notice? He hoped so.

'I suppose one more drink wouldn't hurt…' – she had definitely noticed, he thought. 'Okay, I'll have the same again… please, Jack.' A polite girl – Jack liked that. He signalled to the barman to make Belle's a double – it would be easier that way. Looking up from her phone, she accepted the drink with gratitude before slipping the phone back into her bag, snapping the clasp shut. He had her full attention now.

As 'one more drink' turned into a third, their surroundings dissolved into insignificance. Belle was completely entranced by Jack's humour and charisma – she clung to his every word, like a bee to a honeypot. He undressed her with the intensity of his attentive eyes – stripping back her layers with compliments and forged kindness. He stroked her bare knee with his rough knuckles, suppressing a groan as he relished her supple warmth. 'It's getting late, sweetheart… I should get going.' Stepping down from the stool, he towered over her, nudging between her legs, just slightly. Placing a palm on each tensed thigh, he felt for the hem of her dress, caressing just beneath it with the very tips of his fingers. She wasn't sure how to respond, but she knew that he couldn't leave her, not yet. 'You can share a taxi with me if you want?' He wound his hand around the back of her neck, pulling firmly and branding her lips with a kiss. 'Or, you can come back to mine?' His words trailed into a second kiss – tongue invading her mouth before she could answer.

Good girls don't talk to strangers… but he doesn't feel like a stranger. She agonised over the desires of her heart versus her mind. *Tonight* could be the night; she clung to the hope dangling before her, quashing any reservations before they could sprout and spawn. 'Okay,' she nodded meekly, taking his hand as he helped her balance on her four-inch heels. His fingers grasped her waist as she wavered; a hunger was brewing, with unyielding intensity; fiendish possession taking hold of all rationality. She would be his, tonight.

The sky had blackened and a thick fog had wrapped itself around the city, smothering even the dim amber glow of the streetlights above them. Belle's teeth chattered and she exhaled soft, vaporous clouds, as the autumn chill penetrated her to the bone. Jack held her against his body, sharing his strength, warmth and longing. His hands crawled over her skin and lewdly grasped at her curves. She squirmed against him, sucking in copious mouthfuls of air as she tried desperately to regain clarity of her vodka-hazed mind. He would be hers, tonight.

'Jack… I'd like you to come back to mine instead. Will you?' He was surprised but he liked her confidence. He tilted her chin upwards so her eyes would look into his, and the iridescent light of the crescent moon illuminated the right-hand side of her face. He noted soft creases at the corners of her eyes – perhaps marking age or experience he hadn't seen there before, he wondered.

'Will your parents be home?' He glared down at her.

'You know what I need, don't you, sweetheart?' She giggled, nibbling his lip playfully.

'They've gone away,' she replied, leading him by the hand towards a taxi. 'Gone…' she repeated, sliding into the taxi's back seat and tugging him closer by his tie. He climbed in after her, slamming the door closed, locks snapping down.

* * *

The clouds overhead thickened and rolled closer with a rumble as the taxi pulled up outside the house. Stepping out, Jack looked up in awe, taking in the impressive façade of the secluded grey-brick house. In the highest placed window, a small light was visible through a crack in the curtains, but the rest of the rooms were completely dark. There was a heavy air of neglect to the house's garden. He scanned the unkempt wiry bushes, and amongst the wilderness of uncut yellowing grass and weeds, he noted a disused wooden swing set. The seat was fractured and the ropes frayed. It creaked as the wind playfully pushed it, breathing a fleck of life into the lonely scene before him.

They went inside, and he thrust her, with passionate force, against the hallway wall and pushed his hand up her dress, causing it to bunch around her waist. Dropping her belongings with a clatter, she fingered the wall, feeling for the light switch. The sight of her pink lace knickers released the primal hound from its cage. Taking her slim wrists and pinning them above her head, he hissed into her ear, 'Are you going to be a good girl?' She yanked and wriggled, but he held her still with ease – his entire body pressing into hers, taking the satisfaction he so desperately needed.

'I'm always a good girl, Daddy.' She grinned into his narrowing eyes – catching him off guard. As he processed her choice of words, she seized her opportunity and deftly slipped free from his grip, ducking under his arm. She snatched up her keys and locked and bolted the door, before tucking them away in the smallest drawer of the wooden sideboard. She pulled her dress back down her thighs and smiled into the mirror as she wiped away all remaining traces of smudged lipstick. Belle enjoyed watching Jack pant in frustration – it excited her. 'We've got all night,' she assured him. 'Now come and have a drink with me.'

Taking Jack by the hand, she guided him through to the living room. She gently pushed him back into the moss-green, highbacked armchair that was there by the fireplace. 'This is Daddy's seat – you'll like it.' The chair was firmer than it had looked, and somehow, it felt bitterly cold against his back and thighs, sending chills coursing through his veins. Belle kissed his cheek. 'Make yourself at home,' she said and disappeared behind him. He heard the sound of ice and glasses clinking, and he glanced at his watch. It showed the time as 12.05 and was ticking melodically as it should, but the second hand remained perfectly still. He tapped at the face, but that didn't help – the second hand didn't move on. He would need to get that looked at.

With a sigh, he pulled himself up from the chair and moved to explore the room. As though an indiscernible force were tugging him there, he found himself drawn to the fireplace – more specifically, to the photographs that adorned the mantelpiece. He ran his fingers along the edge of the first frame, smudging away a thick layer of dust to reveal the jewelled embellishment. Inside the frame, there was a photograph of a man and girl who was aged about five or six. Jack was sure the girl must be Belle. In the photo, which had yellowed a little with age, she was sitting on the old swing, legs dangling as she clasped the ropes with both hands. She was wearing a frilly white summer dress and had her hair in red ribbons. The girl in the photo glared back at him with those same eyes she had stared at him with tonight – eyes which seemed to burn into his conscience. His attention travelled to the man who stood beside her. He looked to be in his mid-thirties and he was dressed in a smart suit – navy in colour like the one he himself was wearing tonight. Hollowness consumed the man's features. Jack couldn't take his eyes away from the sallow eyes and drawn cheeks. His lifeless fingers seemed to call out to Jack, as if to warn him to leave—

'What are you doing?' Belle startled Jack, interrupting his thoughts; the frame slipped from his fingers and landed face down on the mantel. 'I told you to sit down, didn't I?' she said brusquely, before adding, with a sickening sweetness that unnerved Jack, 'Sit in Daddy's chair.' As she slowly approached him, with two crystal tumblers of whisky over ice, he bit his tongue – after all, she still looked incredible in her figure-hugging dress and black stiletto heels. He knew that he just needed to regain control of the situation. He had come for one thing only and he certainly didn't intend on leaving without it.

As he relaxed back into the chair, he had the strangest feeling that the cushions were imprinted with the form of another. Belle handed him a glass, pushing her own into the centre of the coffee table. She moved onto Jack's lap, slowly grinding against him as she made herself comfortable. Her arms snaked possessively around his neck and he began to kiss her shoulder, placing one arm around her hip, caressing her thigh.

She tore away from his advances. 'You didn't say thank you for your drink.'

'Thanks,' he mumbled in annoyance. With a theatrical gesture, he acknowledged his gratitude towards her, tilting his glass and swallowing down a large gulp. He ended up taking a larger gulp than he meant to, and he winced as it flooded his throat and warmed him through to the pit of his stomach. There was an acrid taste left on his tongue – an aftertaste of burnt cinnamon or bitter melon? Had the whisky gone bad, been stored open for years or something? – she didn't look like the whisky-drinking type, after all.

Belle nodded and smiled, moving his hand to her inner thigh, parting her legs a little further. Eagerly, he tried to thrust towards her honeypot, but she clamped his hand with her own…

'Kiss my forehead and say thank you, baby girl.' Reluctantly he obliged, and in return, she removed her hand from his, allowing his fingers to skim the lace of her damp underwear. Her moans were the enchanting song of a Siren – seducing and enthralling Jack, lulling him closer and closer to complete desperation. He needed her now; he needed to ravage her completely. She pressed the glass to his lips and tipped it gently. 'Drink up – I want to show you my bedroom.'

'Now you're being a good girl,' he laughed emptily,

placing down the tumbler and losing his fist in Belle's thick, dark hair as he gripped roughly and kissed her. As she stood up to guide Jack towards the stairs, pins and needles prickled up and down his back and thighs. *Stupid fucking chair*, he cursed, silently.

The upstairs landing was pitch black, bar the single fuzzy strip of light that shone from under the farthest doorway. Belle led him by the hand, and the sound of her heels on the wooden floor resonated through the house. The hallway felt as though it were growing in length and yet it seemed to constrict with every step he took – the walls were closing in around him. It was stiflingly warm and he struggled to take in more than a shallow gasp with each inhalation. Jack loosened his tie and unbuttoned the topmost button on his shirt. Belle let go of his hand and skipped ahead with childlike zest, throwing open the door and flooding light into Jack's path. He winced as his eyes adjusted to the brightness. His forehead was burning now and his stomach clenched painfully – he already knew that he was going to regret that last whisky in the morning. He should have known better.

Belle kicked off her heels and headed over to the four-poster bed in the centre of the room. 'Come and join me!' she squealed, excitedly. Apprehensively, he entered the candy-pink playroom, taking in the fairy lights around the window, the doll's house and the mountain of stuffed toys in the far corner. He pulled at his tie with increasing desperation as a cold surge washed over his body. His shirt clung uncomfortably as sweat ran down his back. Belle's voice became nothing more than a ringing in his ear.

Hot.

Cold.
Tight.
Weak.

A pulsing tremor took hold of his right leg, seizing and spreading from ankle to thigh – then pounding and consuming the entirety of his left leg also. Jack forced himself to stagger towards the bed. Belle helped Jack to drag his carcass onto the centre of the bed, guiding him into the comforting hold of the throw cushions. He sank back, gasping as his mouth began to dry and his tongue began to feel like a thick, leather belt, coated in the acrid taste of burnt cinnamon. As the room began to spin uncontrollably around him, he closed his eyes and stroked the smooth indentation on his ring finger with the pad of his thumb.

'It won't be long now,' Belle cooed into his ear, straddling his lap. She took a wooden paddle brush and brushed his dishevelled hair with it, using long tender strokes to comb his hair in a neat side parting. 'You need to look smart, Daddy…' she tutted, buttoning his shirt and shuffling his tie back to the top, with a choking tug.

'Belle… what the…' Jack tried to scream out, but the words clotted in his throat and exited as a feeble whisper. He tried to kick, he tried to stand, but a paralytic numbness was dispersing through every inch of his body with unstoppable intensity. As the toxins coursed through his veins like wildfire, Jack's heart thumped and leapt with sheer fright. Like a drop of the darkest ink spreading through water, stillness took hold of his body. Slowly, the outward shaking and panic dissipated, until finally, he roared, but he did not move. He cried out but only silent tears slid from the corners of his eyes. He was a captured animal, ripe and ready for slaughter. He was powerless.

As she mopped his damp brow and kissed his cheek, his eyes moved frantically around the room, but there was no help and no escape. He looked at the shelf of porcelain dolls, all lined up, ready and willing to play her games. Their eyes burned through him as the last few ounces of courage drained from him and he felt the life leaving the extremities of his body. He was soon completely numb. His eyes finally settled upon the *Beauty and the Beast* clock hanging silently on the wall, motionless at 12.05. Silence and stillness settled throughout the house.

'You'll make the best daddy in the world,' she smiled sweetly, sinking down and snuggling up against his chest. She wrapped her arms around him and placed her leg over his. She lay contentedly, listening to the throbbing of his heart as it beat in time to the ticking of his watch; tick, tick, ticking - but never moving forward. 'You're the best daddy in the world because you'll never leave me.'

ANGEL HAIR

Deborah Sheldon

The river overflowed a few times every year, but this time it was different. Amy woke often during that final night. She would startle as if from a bad dream and listen to the sop and sigh of the floodwaters lapping against the house until her heart slowed and she could drowse again. The digital clock remained blank, meaning the house was still without electricity, but at sixteen years of age, she wasn't scared of the dark anymore. When she woke and noticed daylight around the curtains, she sat up. Something was wrong. It took her a moment to figure it out.

The silence.

The utterly profound silence.

All the outside noises had gone. No bubble and burble of floodwater, which was a good thing, since it meant the river had receded and her parents, stranded at their butcher's shop in town, could now come home. But no sounds of traffic either, no Saturday morning music from the neighbour's house, no barking dogs or crowing roosters, no bird calls, no wind sighing through the trees. Amy got out of bed. The silence pressed around her, thickly, as if she were underwater.

She opened the curtains.

What she saw didn't make sense.

The five acres of their rural property should be covered in autumn leaves, not snow. And when had it ever snowed in this part of Victoria? Not in Amy's lifetime. Yet the snow must have been a metre thick on the ground.

'Grandpa?' she called behind her. 'Are you awake?'

He didn't answer.

An early riser, perhaps he was downstairs already, out of earshot.

Amy stared again out the window. At first glance, yes, it had appeared to be snow, but now she wasn't so sure. Could it be fog? Some bizarre weather anomaly triggered by the flood? Her bedroom overlooked the fruit trees. They should be bare, yet they were lost beneath a giant sheet, buried, an orchard of smothered white humps, row upon interlocked row. The gauze that stretched between each tree reminded Amy of the netting her parents would throw over the canopies in summer to keep the birds from pecking holes in the apricots and peaches. But that unnatural, pale mesh wasn't snow, fog or netting.

What the hell was it?

Amy's heart thumped. The pane must be dirty, tricking her eyes. She turned the latch and lifted the sash window.

Oh God. The air smelled unwashed and musky, a complex mix of sweet, sour and rancid notes. Recoiling, pressing a hand against her nose and mouth, she went to shut the window. But then, against the clear and sharp blue of the sky, she saw them: a mess of long, dangling threads, each one finer than a human hair, glistening in the early morning light, twisting in the breeze, showering down by the thousands, by the hundreds of thousands, a silent rainstorm.

Transfixed, Amy watched.

It was an eerie yet beautiful sight.

A raft of streamers blew in through the window. They swept over her, sticky and wiry. Insects, she just knew it, *shit*, they were moving over her. With a shriek, Amy slammed the window closed. She slapped and swiped at her face and hands, and ripped off her pyjamas, throwing them to the floor. She leaned in for a closer look. Countless spiders swarmed her pyjamas, so tiny that dozens might fit on a button. Alarmed, disgusted, Amy stamped the fabric, over and over.

Jesus.

Gasping, she pulled on a T-shirt and jeans. She had to find Grandpa. Then she saw the closed window. The glass was frosted with silk, and crawling with spiders.

'Grandpa!' she yelled. 'Where are you?'

'Downstairs.'

She raced to the mezzanine. The door to her parents' bedroom stood open, the bed still unslept in and neatly made. She took the stairs two at a time. The ground floor stank of mould and swamp. She reached the kitchen. Her bare feet landed in a centimetre or so of cold floodwater. A muddy line along the walls showed the waters had peaked at knee-height. The ground floor was in disarray: the entry-table on its side, wet sofa cushions piled up against the front door, twigs and leaves thick over the boards, random shoes scattered like beached fish.

Grandpa stood up from the kitchen table and smiled, patting the air with both hands as if to shush her.

'Everything is all right,' he said. 'It's only angel hair.'

'Angel hair?'

'It happens sometimes after a flood. Instead of drowning, baby spiders throw out a line of web and float away on the wind like this, see?' He waved his hand through the air, wiggling his fingers. 'It's a kind of migration. Now take a seat. I'll make you breakfast.' He went to the stove and clicked the burner. 'At least the gas still works. Omelette?'

She nodded, sat at the table, and looked out the back door, which was a sheet of glass set alongside a floor-to-ceiling window. Normally, she would see a brick path lined with Mum's rosebushes. Instead, there were billions of white, cross-hatching silk threads, and the wriggling black dots of the spiders that made them.

She said, 'It looks like the end of the world.'

'Not everything's a zombie apocalypse. Notice how quiet it is? The webbing soaks up the sound waves.'

'It's creepy. I don't like it.'

'No one said you had to.' He cracked eggs into a pan and began to whisk. 'If you think this is bad, you should have seen Esperance back in, oh, sometime in the nineties. I happened to be there on business. The angel hair covered about a hundred square kilometres, believe it or not. Spiders floated so high, they even got stuck on aeroplanes. But the webs were gone by next morning. Angel hair leaves the way it comes, like magic. You want herbs?'

'Okay,' she said. Another drift landed against the glass. The spiders seemed intent, determined, angry. 'When do you think we'll hear from Mum and Dad?'

'As soon as the landline comes back on, I expect.

They're probably staying at the motel and having a grand old time.'

Amy didn't reply. Her mobile was dead too. She and Grandpa were cut off. The pile of silks and spiders against the glass was growing higher. She became aware of a strange noise coming from all around: a flittering against the roof, walls and windows, a whisper that seemed to be getting louder.

Grandpa put the omelette in front of her, with a knife and fork.

'Are we going to be okay?' she said.

'Sure we are. Now tuck in.'

She ate but mechanically, hardly noticing each mouthful. Angel hair piled up on the door and window like snowflakes driven by the wind, yet there was no wind. She watched Grandpa lean against the servery bench and stare at the phenomenon. He began to frown, gnaw at his lips. Amy's stomach tightened. Finally, he took his glasses from his shirt pocket and put them on.

'Look at that,' he said, jolting, and pointed a finger. 'You see that?'

He was pointing at the frame around the back door. Yes, she saw it. The house was old, had settled over the years, and the doors and windows didn't fit squarely within their frames. Gaps that let in the draughts were now letting in the spiders. Webbing bulged and foamed. Scores of little arachnids broke away from the foam and eddied on their long, cotton-like strands across the kitchen. They were floating towards Amy and Grandpa.

Grandpa took the fly spray from the pantry. 'Cover your omelette.'

He fired a stream of fly spray around the door and

window frames. The chemical stink made Amy want to sneeze. Angel hair drooped wetly.

'There,' Grandpa said. 'That'll fix 'em.'

Gossamer threads drifted into her field of vision. She turned in her chair. From the ventilation slots high in the wall swelled a great bubble of silk, with spiders breaking off and showering the air.

'There's more,' she said. 'Up there.'

He shook the can and sprayed the ventilation slots.

'Let's check the rest of the house,' he said. 'You ought to be wearing shoes. Christ knows what the floodwaters have left behind.'

She found a muddy pair of runners and pulled them on. Grandpa had already left for the lounge room. She hurried after him, the rubberised soles of her runners squeaking and squealing against the wet floorboards, the only sound apart from the feathery fall of angel hair against the house.

With a hand to her mouth, Amy stopped dead.

Grandpa stood in the middle of the lounge, stunned, the can of fly spray held by his side, forgotten. The half-dozen sash windows frothed with angel hair. Great clumps kept breaking off and releasing puffs of spiders. Each puff directed itself towards them. Amy experienced a moment of clarity: the creatures must be sharing a consciousness, acting in concert like the cells of a single animal.

'Let's go,' she said, dragging Grandpa by the wrist.

The laundry had a single fixed window and no ventilation slots. Amy slammed the door behind them. For the next minute, she and Grandpa crushed all the spiders they could find on themselves and each other.

When they finished, they were both covered in tiny spots of spider guts.

'What's going on?' Grandpa muttered. 'Some kind of plague?'

'We need to fumigate every room.'

From the cupboard, Amy brought out packet after packet of bug bombs, which Grandpa lined up on the lid of the washing machine. At certain times of the year, the house suffered from cockroach infestations. Dad preferred to deal with the problem himself rather than call in a pest control company. God, were her parents okay?

Grandpa said, 'We've got enough chemicals here to sink a ship.'

'If we hide in the bathroom and chock the door with wet towels, we'll be fine. We can hold out for hours with running water and a toilet.'

Grandpa suddenly looked older, as if his skull had shrivelled inside his flesh. The sight unnerved her. She pulled towels from the hamper and gave one to him.

'Put this over your head,' she said. 'You do the ground floor. I'll do upstairs. We'll meet in the downstairs bathroom, all right?'

They both left the laundry. Amy took the stairs. As she hurried from room to room, setting each bug bomb, the fogs of swirling gossamer threads seemed to chase after her. Impossible. She must be disturbing the air with her passage, drawing the gossamer in her wake. Threads stuck to her. Whenever she wiped her hands along the backside of her jeans, she felt the crack of exoskeletons.

The stink from the hissing bug bombs started to choke her.

She had to hurry, go faster, faster.

The carpets crawled with spiders, popping softly in their hundreds with her every footfall. When she reached the stairs again, grabbing the banister and looking down to make sure of her step, she flinched.

Both feet were swathed in webs. Swarms of spiders charged up her legs.

She bounded down the stairs. Hysteria broke a long, wailing scream out of her. Once in the bathroom, she ripped the towel from her head and used it to beat at her jeans. Spiders flew in every direction. They scattered over the tiled walls, scampered across the floor, ran around inside the bath, the sink, drowned within the toilet bowl. The can of fly spray was in the laundry. Why hadn't she thought to bring it with her?

Amy's breath came and went in ragged, jagged gulps.

Stop it.

Get a grip.

But in the mirror, she saw wriggling black dots all over her.

She turned on the shower and stood under it, fully clothed, the water ice-cold. The spiders sluiced away in sheets and whirled in clots, thick as mud, down the plughole. *Get off me, get off me, get off me…* She kept scrubbing at her hair, T-shirt and jeans with clawed hands, until the water ran clear.

Now what? The bathroom was infested.

She got out of the shower, flushed the toilet over and over, and ran the taps in the sink and bath to swish the tiny monsters down the drains. Wetting the towel she had worn on her head, she wiped at the floor and walls, and then flung the towel into the still-running shower and shut the glass door. Only a few spiders remained, high on the walls, on the ceiling… Amy's breathing started to slow down.

Everything was okay; she was okay. She was dripping wet, shivering, but at least she wasn't covered in spiders, and everything was okay. Except…

Except, where was Grandpa?

Dread prickled at her nerves. She opened the bathroom door a crack, put her mouth to it and yelled, 'Grandpa!'

No answer.

She closed the door. What should she do? Wait? Go out and look for him? He might have had a heart attack. Or he may have been overwhelmed by spiders. Right now, they might be cocooning him, stopping his nose and mouth with silk.

The towel in the shower recess was sopping. She wrung it out and put it over her head. If only she had that goddamned fly spray. Bracing herself, she tightened her grip on the doorknob. On the count of three…

One… two…

'Open up!' Grandpa yelled.

His weight thumped against the door. Amy let him in. He was covered in webs and scraping at his eyes. She manhandled him under the shower and helped him rinse off the spiders. When the water ran clear, he shut off the tap. She gave him a dry towel from the rack. They stared at each other for a few moments. Amy imagined that her own face must look as grey and frightened as Grandpa's. Slowly, absent-mindedly, he began to dry his head and hands. Amy watched him, her heart pounding.

Movement caught her eye. Scuttling under the door

were more hordes. She stamped on them, then dropped her wet towel and pushed it against the door.

Grandpa began to nod. He said, 'The authorities will take care of this. Don't worry. Any minute now, we'll hear fire trucks, police sirens, alarms.'

They sat down together on the edge of the bath. Amy reached for his hand. Grandpa interlaced their fingers. During the two hours they waited for the bug bombs to work, they didn't hear anything but the continuous, soft pelting over the house.

Grandpa looked at his watch. 'Let me check,' he said at last, and exited the bathroom. Within seconds, he was back, eyes wild. 'We've got to leave.'

'Huh? What about the bug bombs?'

'There's too many.'

The sound on the roof and weatherboards wasn't muffled anymore. No, it was loud, like pattering rain, a steady and relentless drizzle, the kind of drizzle that threatens to become a downpour. The frosted glass of the window looked white.

'I'll get my car,' Grandpa said. 'I'll drive it out front so you can hop in.'

The garage wasn't attached to the house. It was a half-minute walk from the porch across open ground.

'But the spiders,' she said. 'How will you reach the garage?'

He frowned, tugged at an earlobe. 'Well, I guess I'll put on a raincoat, gumboots, take an umbrella. Once you're in the car, we'll drive to town and find out what the hell's going on.' He seemed to consider this for a moment, and added, 'We might have to drive further, perhaps to the city. I'm not sure. God only knows how much angel hair is falling. Maybe it's not angel hair after all.'

He nodded to himself, as if making up his mind, and draped a towel over his head. Panicked, Amy gripped his hand. It felt cold.

'Don't go,' she said.

He shook his hand free. 'When you hear the car horn, run to the front door.'

'Let me come with you.'

'I won't be long,' he said, taking hold of the doorknob. 'Keep an ear out. I'll lean on the horn.'

He kissed her, a peck on the forehead, and then closed the door behind him, but not quickly enough to stop the flurry of incoming spiders. Amy beat them to the floor with a towel and trod on them. The acrid stink from the bug bombs had wafted in too. After a while, she sat on the edge of the bath and listened for the car horn. There was no clock in the bathroom. How much time had already passed?

She began counting.

One *cat-dog*, two *cat-dog*, three *cat-dog*...

When she reached five hundred *cat-dog* and Grandpa still hadn't sounded the horn, Amy draped a towel on her head, and left the bathroom.

Her home resembled a Halloween-styled haunted mansion. The webbing on the walls, from floor to ceiling, created round tunnels throughout every room. Dead spiders crunched underfoot like powdered snow. The live spiders were slow, drowsy, affected by the bug bombs.

Amy ducked into the laundry for the fly spray. From the cupboard by the front door, she took out her gumboots, raincoat and umbrella. She sprayed each item liberally, and put the can in the deep pocket of her raincoat. The car horn still hadn't sounded. Amy didn't want to think about this too much. She put on the raincoat, slipped the gumboots over her runners, and unfurled the umbrella. Thrusting her hand into webbing, she flung open the front door and stumbled onto the porch.

Her breath hitched.

The outside world had disappeared. In its place lay a single, endless, smothering blanket. Trillions of spiders dropped from a giant cloud. In the distance, the familiar sights of sky, horizon and earth were gone, replaced by a grey and billowing mist. Aghast, lifting the umbrella, Amy hurried to where the garage ought to be. Was the spider-rain getting thicker, heavier? Had the spiders sensed her?

'Grandpa!' she yelled.

The webbing swirled about her legs with each step, as if she were wading through cotton candy. Spiders poured in their hundreds off the umbrella. She was close enough now to see the garage. The double doors stood open. Grandpa had made it that far. Staggering, panting, Amy ran inside the garage. Her eyes took a few moments to adjust to the dimness. Then she saw it and dropped the umbrella.

On the floor, shrouded like an Egyptian mummy, lay a human shape.

Spiders scuttled across the cocoon. Amy emptied the fly spray over them. The arachnids shrivelled. Collapsing to her knees, weeping, she ripped at the cocoon with both hands. At last, she tore away the silk from Grandpa's face. His staring eyes crawled with spiders. Webs filled his open mouth.

She fell back to the concrete floor, retching, whimpering.

Angel hair crept up her limbs.

She clawed at Grandpa's cocoon and found the car keys in his hand. Amy had her learner permit, had taken a few driving lessons with Dad, but her fear wasn't in operating Grandpa's old Commodore. No, it was in keeping to the long, winding driveway when she couldn't see the bitumen. Near the front gate, the driveway ran over a creek. She would have to negotiate the bridge. If she put the car into the creek, she'd never get it out again.

Once inside the car, Amy took off the raincoat and gumboots. She had brought spiders in with her, but she crushed as many as she could with her fingers. She started the engine. Pulses drummed madly throughout her body. She put the car into 'drive' and coasted out of the garage and into the webs.

The car's passage made cracking, shearing, creaking, rending noises, which made her shiver in revulsion. Angel hair soon covered the windscreen. The wipers mashed and smeared it into grey paste. Amy leaned over the steering wheel, squinting, searching for landmarks. The angel hair that had gathered at the bumper began to creep up and across the bonnet. What if the radiator overheated?

Don't think about it.

The sound of spiders hitting and sliding over the roof scraped at her nerves. She put on the radio. It was an old-timey song, from a station that Grandpa liked. Tears pricked. She snapped off the radio. Grandpa was dead because of her. She should have gone with him. She should have insisted…

There!

The sight galvanised her. There, the railings of the bridge, she could see them. She would make it after all. She would drive to town and find her parents. Together, they would head for the city and away from this nightmare. The tyres smushed over angel hair, yet she could still hear the rhythmic *drub-dub drub-dub* of the bridge's wooden planks. She scrubbed away the tears on her cheeks.

She reached the highway. Or did she? It was difficult to tell. The neighbouring houses, the petrol station, the milk bar, the buildings which should be right in front of her, were reduced to gauzy lumps. And further back lay an impenetrable fog where the vineyard should be, and the hills beyond it, and the sky.

The car's engine coughed, wheezed. The red needle of the temperature gauge rose as she looked at it. Sweat trickled from her hairline. A few stray spiders tickled at the back of her neck. She turned the steering wheel, ploughed on.

Was she on the highway or not?

Something lay ahead, something large. As she got closer, she recognised its shape. It was a sedan, completely cocooned. Were people trapped inside? Yes, there would have to be at least a driver. Amy sounded the horn.

No response.

Maybe the driver had ditched and made a run for it.

Carefully, she steered around the sedan. Her armpits felt clammy, her mouth dry. She put the windscreen wipers on top speed and flicked the lever for the washers, trying to clear the angel hair. She feared crashing into a ditch. Every now and then, she spotted the mound of a roadside post, and adjusted her course.

Tiny arachnids gathered at the edges of the windows, as if trying to find a way inside. Cars weren't airtight, she knew that. The spiders would get inside. They would find a way. Her legs felt itchy. From real or imagined spiders? She couldn't afford to check. She had to keep both hands on the wheel. The webbing pulled and dragged at the tyres. Her foot was flat to the boards, yet she was travelling at only twelve kilometres per hour, now eleven, now ten, as if she were driving into a bog.

Up ahead were more cocooned vehicles.

Amy leaned on the horn. No answering honk came back.

There was just silence, an utterly profound silence out there, and the whisper of angel hair as it landed and collected itself on the car.

THERE IS A MAN IN EDITH'S HOME

Sam Rebelein

There is a man in Edith's home. She can't remember inviting him in here, but that's no surprise. Edith was diagnosed with a brain thing last fall. She remembers *that*, but not what the thing is called. She remembers that she can't remember things.

Sometimes.

She drifts into the living room and sees this man sitting on her couch, staring at her TV. It's night. The room is dark except for the lamp on the side table and the glow of the TV. There's a report on Channel 7 about someone who's running around the tri-state area, murdering people and taking their hands. All these bodies found in ditches and road-shoulders and gutters, on their backs with their hands folded over their chests. Well…their ragged stumps, at least.

It's all very exciting, according to the tone of the reporter woman's voice. There hasn't been a serial killer *this* good since the 80s. Edith can tell, because they keep throwing the phrase "serial killer" around with increasing severity.

What a ridiculous thing. What would anyone want with

all those hands? Where would you keep them? The freezer?

This young man shouldn't be watching all that crap. It'll give him nightmares. Edith wants to tell him that, but she might not have a right to. Maybe he's her adult son, and he can watch whatever he likes. Or he might laugh her off, like the mean nurse with the CPAP machine used to. He used to laugh at her all the time, tell her, "We *just* talked about this, Edith. Get your brain under control, girl." And then his machine would whirr all night, keeping Edith awake.

That'd driven her *nuts*. She's happy he's gone, though she can't remember what happened to him. She hopes nothing *bad*. Edith might've hated him, but she'd never wish ill on anyone. Would she? She hopes she just asked for someone new, but she can't remember doing that. Nor can she remember who her nurse now is.

Edith watches this man for a bit. She can only see the back of his head, haloed by the TV. This head has brown hair. Edith has brown hair. Or…had. Is this her son?

She looks around the kitchen, hoping to ask the live-in nurse (the mean one…or is he gone?) who this man is. She can't ask *him*, the man himself. That would be embarrassing. Edith is in constant fear of embarrassing herself these days. She can't remember, but she thinks she's hit on her son before, finding him very handsome without remembering who he is. She doesn't want to do that again.

But she doesn't see the nurse in the kitchen. She doesn't remember *who* she's supposed to see, which nurse, but nobody's there at all, so.

She pads back down the hall, her bare old feet making

soft sliding noises along the carpet. She creaks open the door of the spare bedroom. She peers inside. The room is void of the mean nurse's stuff. In the room is Edith's mother's rocking chair and the bed, neatly made, Edith's pink quilt draped finely across it. The nurse's suitcase, Kindle, CPAP machine—all are gone.

Did she get a new nurse?

But then she recognizes her son's duffel bag flopped across the bed. She bought that for him for his first job after college, when he was traveling to Albany a lot.

So that *is* her son on the couch! Maybe he's moved in. Maybe there *is* no nurse anymore.

What's her son's name again? Good grief, the shock of realizing she can't remember isn't even a shock anymore. She can't call him Jeremy, that was her husband's name. She's made that mistake before. She *must* remember that. "You *must* remember, Edith," she tells herself.

"Hello?" the man calls. He sounds startled. And again, more firmly, "Hello."

Edith doesn't recognize the voice, but it *must* be her son. Who else would it be?

She edges back out of the bedroom and closes the door. It creaks. Clicks.

"M…mom?"

Edith is embarrassed. She should have *known* this is her son. Damn her brain for not remembering! She pads back down the hall, towards her room. But then her room isn't there. There's just a closet. In fact, this isn't her hall. Wait a minute. That wasn't her spare bedroom.

Is this her house? She'd thought it was hers because all the pictures on the walls are familiar. But now that she looks closely at them, she realizes they're just her son and his family. Is she in *his* house? That's why there's no nurse—she's living with her son.

She can hear the man mute the TV, shove himself off the couch, and start walking quickly after her, down the hall. The hall light clicks on. Edith ducks into a bedroom she doesn't recognize (or is this hers?), and tucks herself into the shadows in the corner.

"Mom?" There's an odd tinge to her son's voice that she can't quite read. Does he sound sad? Scared? "Mom."

She doesn't know what time it is. It's dark outside. Should she be asleep? She stands awkwardly in the corner, hands pressed to the wall, wreathed in night and the blades of pale moonlight slicing through the shaded window.

The man stands in the doorway, lit from behind so she cannot see his face. He looks around. He looks at her. They stare at each other, not moving. Can he see her?

He shakes his head. "Jesus…" And goes back down the hall, sighs onto the couch, and continues watching TV.

Edith has really embarrassed herself this time.

She sneaks out through the open window.

* * *

Edith discovers a load of meat inside the fridge. Meat and other food. Trays of sausage and cheese, big Tupperware things of casserole and potato salad, coleslaw. There's plastic-wrapped sandwiches. And some paper packages of what Edith thinks might be steak or chicken. It's raw and in strips. Pulled pork?

Edith has obviously missed a big event. Was she

supposed to host it? Did she? How did it go? How many days have passed? Is that man still here?

She closes the fridge. It's nighttime, and she's in this house again. This time, she can tell it's not her house. She recognizes the kitchen and the hallway from before. Except everything's darker now. All the lights are off. There's a chill. Edith sees a window open in the living room. She shuts it. Who left that open? It's not good. There's a giant hole in the screen. A whole person could crawl through.

She creeps down the hall and eases open her son's door. It creaks. The man is in bed with a woman. When Edith creaks open the door, the man bolts upright in bed, clearly startled. "Mom?"

Edith doesn't know what to say.

"Mom!"

The man is out of bed now, coming towards her. "Jesus, Mom, did you walk all the way here?"

She can't see his face, it's all dark and nighttime-y. *Is she his mom?* If she asked, would he tell her the truth, or would he *lie* and make *fun* of her, like that mean nurse with the CPAP machine? He even pretended to burn her with a cigarette once, that awful man. Thank goodness the agency sent that new woman, what's her name, Abby. Or has she not arrived yet? Good grief, Edith is so confused.

Her son is guiding her out of the bedroom. The woman is stirring awake now, too. "What is it? Your mom's here?"

"Mom," says the man, "you have to *stop* breaking into my home."

He is gripping her very tightly. She doesn't like the way

his fingers feel, digging into her. Doesn't like it at all.

"Jeremy, stop," she tells him.

He loosens his grip significantly. He sighs. "God. I'm sorry, Mom. I didn't mean to *hurt* you, I just…"

But then Edith is washing her hands in her kitchen again. She dries them calmly, like someone who has just realized they're too drunk for their own good. When she tucks the washcloth back into the stove handle, she happens to look down and see that she's wearing black.

Why is she wearing black?

Then it hits her: the food in the fridge is from the wake.

So…why was she at a wake?

* * *

The man (her son?) has spread all of Edith's old photographs and bills and insurance information on the dining room table. That feels *very* invasive. He would've had to dig under Edith's bed for some of that. When did he do all this, while she was sleeping? Good lord, Edith doesn't even *remember* sleeping. She's lost time again.

Why does her son have all these photographs of *her* spread around? It looks like he's making picture boards. Like she is dead.

Or…were these *her* picture boards? That can't be, she wouldn't be making these things for her *own* funeral…

…would she?

Edith has the sudden fear that she is dead. She's forgotten she's died, and now she's haunting her son's home. The wake—was hers.

She's so upset and embarrassed by this entire thing

that Edith scatters the papers and pictures off the table. She even tears some of them up, into little pieces. Then she's on a roll, so she starts throwing open cabinets and cupboards and drawers. She doesn't break anything else, not after ripping up those papers, but she *does* leave the house in total disarray.

When the man returns from wherever he is, he'll be sorry. Sorry he dug his grubby hands into her things, snooped around and fussed with her stuff.

But when he does return, the man has backup. He has a woman with him, and a little girl. As they're coming through the door, the man is saying something to the girl: "Because Grandma doesn't know where she is, sweetie, and…"

And then they see the house.

Edith hides and waits while they clean everything up. Jeremy calls the agency, speaks with the police. He says Edith has "wandered off." Again.

How ridiculous. Edith is right here!

The family orders pizza, and the next thing Edith knows, the man is in Edith's bed reading something on his iPad, and the woman is tucking the girl into bed in the spare room.

Where is Edith supposed to sleep? This is *her* house. She's been ceding power to this man on the off-chance he's her son, but what if they're just some random people taking advantage of her? What if he's squatting in her home knowing she's just some crazy old lady who'll let it happen?

Edith has forgotten her theory that she is dead.

When they're all asleep, Edith creeps up along the man's side of the bed. She leans down, which is surprisingly easy, given her bad hip. It pops, but it holds steady. And she whispers in the man's ear, "Get...out."

The man bolts upright in bed. "Mom!" he cries. "Mom, is that you!?"

But Edith has already fled back down the hall. For good measure, she smacks the spare room's door as she passes. It swings open with a satisfying *bang*, and the little girl screams.

The man tears through the house calling her name, but Edith is hiding in the wall.

* * *

There is a knock at the door. It's daytime, and Edith is wandering around the house, wondering where the family went. The beds have been slept in, but all their stuff is gone. She's scared them off. It's up to Edith to answer the door.

She does, and the woman there smiles at her. "You must be Edith."

"So I've been told," says Edith. "And who might you be?"

"I'm Anna; I'm your new aid." The woman steps into the house. She sees that it is messy. No one has cleaned up the scraps from the table. No one has closed the cabinet doors. Edith frowns at it all. Didn't the family clean that up yesterday? Or...is this a new mess?

"How long have you been here by yourself?" the woman asks.

"Maybe...only today," says Edith, fidgeting.

"That's a difficult question, I'm sorry."

"No, my son was just here last night," says Edith. "He had his family with him. I...guess they left."

"Oh." Anna, the new nurse, looks concerned. "Last night?"

"Yes. I think."

Anna puts a hand on Edith's shoulder. Edith flinches.

"I'm so sorry to have to remind you of this," says Anna. "Edith…your son's family was killed. Him, his wife, and their daughter. You and I met at the wake? We had the wake *here*. Over a month ago? You… Here."

She goes into the kitchen and opens the fridge. A tremendous odor bursts out, and Anna coughs, buries her nose in the crook of her arm. "See? You still have all the food in there."

She closes the door.

This is something of a relief, talking to this woman, because Edith had truly begun to suspect she was a ghost. If this woman is talking to her, that means she's alive.

But her son…dead. Weeks ago? But she's positive she saw *someone* last night. If it wasn't her son, then who was it?

Or is she conflating memories again? Did that man last night call her *Mom* at all, or…did he say…something else?

"What happened to them?" Edith asks. "My son and…all?"

"That man." Anna shakes her head. "The one who's been stealing hands?"

Edith vaguely remembers this from the news. She thinks she remembers the mean nurse telling her about it, too. Just to scare her.

"Well," says Anna. "That… That's what happened to them."

"So where are the hands?" asks Edith.

"We don't know."

"Oh." Edith chews on this. "That's horrible."

"It is." Anna nods sadly. She takes a big breath. "Let me put my stuff down and I'll make you some tea. Okay?"

She goes down the hall to Edith's spare room with her bags. Edith opens the fridge. The smell is horrible. She can see why the new nurse—was she called Abby? or was it Alma?—gagged a little when she opened the door.

Oops, thinks Edith. She'll need to get rid of that stuff. It's not all *food* per se, and it smells too bad.

Abby will know.

"What are you doing?" Anna asks, smiling.

Edith is standing over the garbage disposal with a fork.

"That's a good question," she admits, laughing.

"It's okay." Anna puts a hand on Edith's shoulder, slips the fork from her grasp. "I'll make the tea." She squeezes Edith's shoulder. "You go sit down."

Edith drifts to the couch. She sits. She waits for the tea.

She doesn't like this new woman. Hannah, is that her name? or was it Amy? She's too handsy, this Amy. She's touched Edith *twice* now, and she's only been here two minutes. Edith doesn't like *anyone* touching her that much. She remembers now—that man's daughter? She kept trying to braid Edith's hair, until Edith couldn't take it anymore. Was that the same girl she saw last night? She remembers someone holding *someone's* hair. Does she have it backwards? Was it Edith holding the girl's hair last night? Was she pulling it hard enough to hurt? That can't be right, and yet... She remembers the girl crying. It was...wet...warm...

Edith can't remember much anymore. She still doesn't

know why there was a man inside her home, or why she has a distinct memory of him (it *was* him, wasn't it?) pacing around in circles on the phone, yelling, "Took my *daughter!*" That woman wailing in the bedroom.

Edith can't remember much, but she has a distinct memory of the mean nurse, coughing blood into his stupid CPAP machine. He looked so peaceful after, when he'd fallen back asleep. Edith remembers crossing his hands over his chest.

"Here you go," says Anna, handing her a steaming mug of greenish water.

Edith takes it, "Thank you," and Anna gives her shoulder another pat, another smile.

Edith smiles back.

Yes, this touching is no good. No good at all.

Edith can't remember much, but she knows one thing for certain. If they're going to get along, this Amy woman and her? Those hands will have to go.

DARLA AND THE CLOWN

MM Schreier

I dabbed at my face with a makeup wipe and grimaced. After three months of wearing heavy clown makeup every day, my skin felt raw. Worst summer job ever. It was supposed to be easy cash before I started grad school, goofing around and making people laugh. Instead, I got an itchy wig, screaming babies, and teenagers who threw peanuts at me. Apparently, not everybody loves a clown.

I sighed and tossed the wipe in the trash. At least it was finally over.

"Hey there Jillian!" One of the acrobat brothers stuck his head into the tent. They were impossible to tell apart. "You need a ride to the wrap party?"

"Nah. My girlfriend, Darla, is picking me up." Butterflies tickled my stomach.

"Oooh, the mysterious Darla! It's about time you brought her around." He waggled his eyebrows at me.

"Yeah, she hates the circus and is afraid of clowns," I snorted.

"That's ironic," he laughed.

The whole anti-clown thing would have been a good thing to know before I had signed the contract. It had ruined my summer. I frowned at the thought. There was more to it than that, but I couldn't put my finger on it. I shrugged and shifted in my seat.

"Well, I'm off." The acrobat smiled and straightened his shirt collar. "You might want to hurry up. This place is going to be a ghost town in about five minutes."

"Save me a drink. Or four."

He laughed and with a wave he dropped the heavy canvas flap, leaving me alone.

I turned back to the dressing table. The sun hovered on the horizon, and the failing light made the tent interior dim. It didn't help that two out of the six light bulbs framing the makeup mirror were out. I'd been asking the foreman for weeks to have them fixed, but the temporary help was on the bottom of the totem pole.

Leaning in, I noticed white smudges lingering in my hairline. Scooching the chair closer, I snatched up another wipe and scrubbed. Never again. I wasn't much of a makeup person, and the white-face foundation was a nightmare to remove.

With a crack, a light bulb exploded in a shower of sparks. I jumped and whipped a protective hand across my face as fragments of glass rained down.

Pop! Pop! Pop!

In quick succession the remaining three blew, plunging the tent into shadow. Heart in my throat, I felt around on the table, searching for my phone.

"Damn it!" A shard bit my fingertip and I yanked back. I shook my hand; the pain was sharp and hot.

With my other hand, I skimmed the tabletop, cautious of the glass. Scrabbling over makeup palettes and blending sponges, it took forever to find the rectangular phone case. I jabbed the flashlight app and sighed in relief as the light snapped on. Inspecting my finger, I found an oozing gash, blood trickling down to the knuckle. I was lucky—there didn't seem to be any glass in the wound. It throbbed though, and I grabbed a tissue to stop the bleeding.

A sense of being watched prickled the hairs on the back of my neck. I aimed the phone, peering into the corners of the tent. The darkness writhed, pulling back from the light. There was no one there. Letting out a shaky breath, I laughed at myself jumping at shadows. It was past time to go.

Pushing the flimsy folding chair back, I glanced up into the mirror. Wide eyes in a pale face stared back at me. Blood from my cut finger splattered the glass, making the reflection appear to bleed from the temple. Gruesome and corpse-like, but familiar like the freeze-frame of one of the horror movies Darla liked to watch. A shudder ran down my spine. I grabbed my purse and fled.

Darla had planned on meeting me at the main gate, opposite the deserted grounds from the employee tents. I skirted the big top and headed across the midway. Everything looked strange in the growing darkness. No carnies hawking their games and cheap trinkets. No ringmaster enticing the guests into the enormous, striped show tent. No flashing lights, no chattering crowds, no raucous music coming from the motionless rides. The absence of the usual chaos was creepy. I picked up my pace.

When the peaked roof of the ticket booth came into view, I uncurled my clenched fists. My palms smarted where the nails had dug into the flesh. Rolling tense shoulders, I glanced behind me and took a last look at the fairgrounds. Good riddance.

Something moved in the shadows.

I froze. My breath hissed between my teeth, my mouth dry. All was still. The silence pressed in on me, heavy as an elephant on my chest. Feet rooted to the ground, I waited for something to happen.

A cold breeze curled around my ankles. An invisible serpent, it slithered between the buildings and whipped dust into a mini cyclone. Something, an object, swirled in its wake. It danced, jumping between the shadows.

Locked knees popped, suddenly too weak to hold my weight and I staggered. Trash. It was only a crumpled newspaper, a piece of trash, blowing in the wind. I hated myself for succumbing to the jitters. Running my hand through my spiky hair, I sighed. I wouldn't tell Darla I'd been so nervous. I couldn't bear the idea of her seeing me as a coward.

I turned my back on the offending bit of newspaper and rounded the corner of the ticket counter. Darla better not be late. I could use a drink, and the wrap party would be going strong by now. Distracted by the thought of an ice-cold microbrew, I ran face first into something tall and metal.

"What the—"

A chain-link fence blocked the main entrance, the end-of-season deterrent against vandals and teenage miscreants. A heavy chain and padlock secured the gate. I rattled the fence and cursed under my breath.

I surveyed the dark fairgrounds behind me. The employee exit was all the way on the other side, beyond the big-top tent. Where I had just come from. Annoyed, I kicked at a stone and it bounced off the fence pole with a hollow thunk. I considered climbing over. In sandals and a skirt. Bad idea.

Peering through the darkness, I looked for Darla's car, but the parking lot was empty. She was late. Something tickled the edge of my memory, but it slipped away like I was grasping at smoke. I shook my head and dismissed the thought.

I fished my phone from my purse to text her. She'd have to meet me in the back lot. Tapping out a message, I pressed send and a red error message popped up on the screen. My stomach flipped. No service. This night was getting better and better.

Squaring my shoulders, I took a deep breath and headed back across the silent grounds. Once again I had the feeling I wasn't alone as I walked through the gaudily painted booths that housed games of skill and chance. I spun around but there were only the abandoned booths. Their only occupants—the impossible to win but highly coveted giant teddy bears—watched me with glass-eyed stares. I hurried on.

At the front of the midway the Ferris wheel towered overhead like a monstrous, skeletal sea urchin. As I stepped beneath its vast shadow, a creak drew my attention up. One of the seats swayed. There was no breeze. The skin of my arms pebbled in gooseflesh.

A second passenger car began to rock, in rhythm with the first. I stepped back as a third and fourth began to move. One by one the dangling chairs picked up speed, until they all jangled in a violent, pulsing wave. The steel frame of the wheel groaned and a bolt worked loose. It clanged down to ricochet off the roof of a nearby lemonade stand. I ducked. The cars vibrated faster.

With a scream of metal, a brace separated from the crossbar and one of the dangling chairs tilted. As if in encouragement, the rest flapped harder, desperate to fly. Frantic, I stumbled back, but my retreat was too late. The slanted car teetered, broke free, and hurtled towards the ground.

I shrieked and scrambled back. My heel turned on a loose stone and I tumbled to the ground. Pain shot through my ankle. Curled in a ball, eyes screwed shut, I braced for the impact. It never came.

Breath ragged, I looked up at the Ferris wheel. It stood, whole and stoic, motionless in the night. The passenger cars were still and quiet. Trembling and confused, I struggled to my feet. My ankle ached where I had twisted it. I pushed through the pain and limped onward. Keep moving.

Ahead, the carousel marked the halfway point to the big top and the employee exit beyond. In daylight, I loved the rainbow-hued prancing horses and sparkling lights. On my break, I would often sit and watch the children circling around and around. Their squealing laughter competed with the cheery music in a raucous symphony.

Wreathed in shadow, the merry-go-round seemed as if it were holding its breath. The air felt heavy and ominous. My feet dragged, unwilling to come too close and disturb the plastic steeds' slumber. I shuffled forward, slow and measured steps, favoring my injured ankle.

Step.

The jingle of harnesses rang out.

Hitch-step.

A horse snorted, pawing the ground.

My uneven footsteps faltered as the carousel burst into life. Flashing lights ran along the base as it began to spin, slow at first. A lively tune played, too loud in the surrounding hush. The horses reared, shaking their manes and rolling their flat, expressionless eyes.

A voice inside my head begged me to move, but I couldn't force my feet to obey. Horrified, I watched the carousel pick up speed. Like a creeping vine, the music wriggled into me, coiling in my chest. It squeezed, compelling my heart to beat in concert with its frenzied tempo. The synthetic mounts galloped, ears laid back and teeth bared.

Tendrils of music probed my mind, trying to take root. It chimed, discordant, making my head fuzzy. A horse screamed. Head in my hands, I tried to order my thoughts. Something important fluttered through my mind, fleeting and skittish. The harder I tried, the further it retreated. Lights blinked on the carousel and thrummed in time with the hypnotic melody. My pulse fluttered. Gasping for breath, I pounced on the elusive thought.

Run!

I wrenched my feet free and lurched forward. Behind me, the carousel fell still and silent.

Fear goaded me onward, hobbling on my good foot. Sweat trickled down my back and ran cold. An icy breeze pursued me, breathing down my neck like a phantom beast. Ahead the white and red big top loomed, a candy-striped behemoth.

Movement caught my eye and I slowed, chest heaving,

and concentrated on the flash of white. A willowy figure with an auburn ponytail sidled between the tent stakes. Relief washed through me.

"Darla?" My voice was a hoarse whisper. The night plucked it from my lips and devoured the sound. The shadowy figure ducked through the opening in the tent and disappeared.

"Darla! Wait!" I hurried after her.

It was pitch black in the tent, and I rummaged in my purse for my phone. Clammy palms slipped on the plastic case. I pressed the home button and a wan square of light illuminated the darkness. Before I could flick on the flashlight app, it faded, battery drained. I swallowed hard.

I strained, listening for footsteps in the heavy silence. The blood rushing in my ears roared like thunder.

"Hello? Darla?" I felt my way along the bleachers. "Is anyone there?"

A whisper floated through the air, the sound of sand shifting underfoot. Someone was moving in the main arena. Warning bells flared in the back of my mind. If it was Darla, why didn't she answer?

My legs moved of their own volition, inching forward. Toes thunked against the low circle of wood and I stepped over the barrier into the center ring. Sand trickled into my sandals, rubbing against my heels.

The hidden eyes were back—watching, measuring. They bored into me, daring me to come closer. A tremor ripped through me and my knees quivered. Gagging on the scent of rotten meat that suddenly seemed to fill the air, I pressed a fist against my mouth and willed down the bile that scorched the back of my throat.

Seconds or hours, time stretched eternal. There was

only my racing heart and the Watcher. In the blackness, the space under the big top felt infinite. A dark abyss, flavored by the scent of my fear. The wraith moved, unseen but felt, drinking in my terror. I cowered.

A spotlight blinded me, and I flung an arm over my eyes.

Look.

The Watcher spoke directly into my mind, using Darla's voice. Compelled, I dropped my arm and opened my eyes.

A music box sat in the sand, topped with a ballerina in a yellow tutu. A chip on the base looked familiar. I frowned; these were puzzle pieces out of place. Mesmerized, I leaned closer. A thrill of foreboding swept through me. Without being wound, the figurine began to twirl, the delicate music tugging on my memory.

Between heartbeats, it all flooded back.

I had scoured the internet trying to find a replica of Darla's cherished childhood treasure—a ballerina music box. She'd lost it in a series of moves and it had broken her heart.

Her face glowed as she opened the box and pulled out the yellow and white figurine, radiant in her delight. She threw her arms around me, her eyes sparkling with unshed tears.

I held her close. Her light was my life. She kept me sane, warded off the darkness. I wanted to feel like this forever.

A second memory eclipsed the first.

A blinding rage had consumed me, blotting out my thoughts. As it faded, I blinked trying to bring the room into focus and catch my breath. Face flushed, I could feel the heft of the music box in my hand, tiny ballet shoes digging into my palm. A crimson smear marred the yellow tutu and the base was chipped. Confused, I set it on the bureau with a frown.

The dresser drawers were open, contents in disarray, and Darla's suitcase lay open at my feet. Was she going somewhere? An ice pick stabbed my head and I rubbed my temples. The pain clarified my thoughts. Darla wasn't just leaving—she was leaving me.

I staggered forward, tripping over something soft. A body lay, crumpled on the floor, arms askew and auburn hair splayed across the carpet. Darla's face was pale and still, blood seeping from her temple. Her lips were rounded in surprise—

The image blanked. Dear God, what had I done?

Guilt crushed down on me and I choked back sobs. I sank to the ground as a wail ripped from my throat. Wrapping my arms around my knees, I rocked back and forth, shoulders shuddering. A presence loomed over me. Judging. I looked up.

The Watcher wore Darla like a mask. Soulless black eyes stared at me from a pallid face, skin sallow, waxy lips tinged gray. She flickered, like a damaged movie reel. Red-black blood matted in her russet waves, trickling down her cheek.

"Oh sweetheart, I'm sorry." The words tasted bitter on my tongue. "I didn't mean it. I was angry."

Her lips pulled back in a mirthless sneer as she reached for me. I tensed. She jerked, disappearing. In the background the music box played on, a haunting, crystalline melody.

Cold hands wrapped around my throat, as Darla's shade reappeared. Her mouth stretched in a silent scream. I grabbed at her wrists, but my hands passed straight through. Fingertips turned numb. Her grip tightened, cutting off my air. My feet scrabbled. I thrashed, unable to find purchase in the shifting sand. A fire raged in my lungs and my vision shrank to a pinpoint.

The tinkling music slowed, and with it the beating of my heart. A vision of Darla, as she had been, floated in memory. Her eyes sparkled as she traced a finger along the figurine's yellow tutu. Notes faltering, the music box wound down. Her vibrant soul guttered, a candle in the wind.

Darla's flame snuffed out. My heart stilled. The last note plunked.

In the silence, the world went dark.

UP FROM THE DARK

Jon Gauthier

The thing's crooked form fills the doorframe. Adam's heart stops for a whisper-thin moment and the familiar terror creeps up his body like a white winter chill. He can only watch as the thing lifts its arm and a serpentine finger uncoils toward him, ancient bones and tendons crackling as they come to life.

He tries to say his wife's name. He feels his lips curl into a tiny sneer and the hiss of an 's' seep through his teeth like steam. Then his mouth opens and forms the rest of the word. It comes out in a desperate asthmatic gasp: "Sarah…"

She can't hear him. The panic takes hold.

"Sarah, it's here. It found me."

He screams, "Sarah!"

The thing moves toward the bed, its face coming into focus like an image through a camera lens: papery grey skin stretched across a weathered and brittle skull; sunken white eyes and a toothless mouth, the whole thing distorted with the desperation of a permanent silent scream.

Wake up, Adam's mind begs, the panic giving way to desperation. *Make it go away.*

"Sarah!"

But he knows she can't hear him because he isn't actually saying anything. Because everything is happening in his mind—his dream. He's having another episode. The paralysis has taken hold again, and it's worse than it's ever been before.

His mind screams—to itself, this time—*Wake up!*

And the thing just drifts toward him.

He tries to lift his arms, but they are welded to the bed. In the conscious part of his mind—the part that floats above the dream—he is able to draw a hand across his chest and drive an elbow into Sarah's side. Then he waits, hoping that the movement has transferred into reality. But Sarah is still and silent beside him, and the thing is right next to him now and bending forward, its vacant ashen face craning towards his. He claws at his subconscious, desperately trying to drag it out of the gloom and force himself awake. Inches away, the toothless mouth opens to an impossible size, revealing an oblivion that stretches beyond nothingness.

The part of him beyond the dream—below him now—pulls his body through the mattress like a catapult, drawing it deeper and deeper into a star-streaked abyss where ghoulish figures swirl and the thing cackles with glee. He pulls and pulls and can feel the rubber bands of his consciousness getting tighter and tighter, stretching to existence-defying thinness.

He screams, *Wake up!* and releases. His head and mind blast up through the murky haze of sleep and his eyes— his real eyes—shoot open as his body bolts into a sitting position. Gasping for breath, he looks around the room. He's relieved to see the thing isn't there.

"Son of a bitch." His voice is flat and lifeless, and a

foul taste sits in his mouth like a dead snake. He looks over at Sarah, who is still sleeping peacefully. He is amazed that she didn't wake up when he did. Hadn't he screamed?

He gets out of bed with a grunt and heads out of the room, opening and closing the French doors as quietly as he can. He's desperate for something to drink, and all he can think about are the small bottles of orange juice currently chilling in the mini bar.

The room is dark, save the moonlight spilling through the balcony door. Adam takes a moment to stop and look out over the Atlantic, which is wide awake— charcoal and silver waves rising and falling onto themselves in an endless churn.

Despite the late hour, the nagging thirst, and the still-raw memory of his recent bout of sleep paralysis, Adam can't help but feel a small sense of joy swell within him. The trip had been wonderful—just the thing he and Sarah needed to reconnect. The deal had seemed too good to be true at first: two nights in a suite at the luxurious Pineloft Ridge Hotel and Nature Spa for only 200 dollars. It was a steal. He'd heard of the place, of course. Who hadn't? But staying there had always seemed like a completely unattainable dream—like visiting the pyramids or Antarctica. So when the email had arrived in his inbox, the one offering him the insanely low rate, he'd leapt at it. A week later, he and Sarah had the Kia packed up and were on their way to the coast.

"Adam?" Sarah's voice, groggy and confused, wanders out of the bedroom.

"Just getting a drink," he calls back to her.

He grabs a bottle of orange juice from the mini bar,

unscrews the cap and swallows a mouthful. It's tepid and tasteless and does nothing to sweeten the sour taste in his mouth—hardly worth the five-dollar price tag. Adam sighs and heads back toward the bedroom.

"Adam?" Sarah's voice again. She sounds concerned now—almost panicked.

He opens the French doors. "I was just getting a—"

A circuit shorts in Adam's brain. The words stop dead in his throat and his entire body goes rigid. Sarah is up on her knees, looking down at a body—his body—lying next to her.

Adam tried to speak—to scream—but his throat won't allow anything to escape.

Sarah screams his name again, "Adam!" She shakes the body violently.

Adam tries to move toward the bed, but he's frozen in place. He manages to let out a single desperate croak, "Sarah…" but it's almost silent.

"Adam, wake up!"

"Sarah!" A scream breaks through, but she doesn't hear it.

"I'll get help," she says with a sob. She begins fumbling with the bedside phone.

Adam cries, "Sarah, I'm here!"

You're still asleep, he thinks. *Just wake up.*

Sarah drops the receiver and almost falls out of the bed trying to pick it up.

Then Adam sees his body's eyes open and instantly realizes that it's the thing from his dream that has opened them. And it's the thing from his dream that's making his body's hand reach for Sarah and touch her shoulder. She lets out a small scream and turns to face the dream thing.

"Oh my god," she gasps, falling into the imposter and wrapping her arms around it. "I thought… I… I couldn't wake you up."

"It's ok, hun," it says as it begins stroking her hair. "I'm here. I'm here, now."

Adam has never called her 'hun'. Not once in six years. She'll notice. She'll know it isn't really him.

"Please, Sarah," Adam begs. "Please hear me."

Then, from over his wife's head, the dream thing locks eyes with him and flashes a porcelain grin.

"What are you?" Adam screams. "How did you find me here?"

It didn't find you here, he thinks. *It brought you here. It's been with you your whole life; guiding you to this very place.*

"Sarah…" Adam's voice is a sobbing whisper now.

"Go back to sleep, hun," he hears the dream thing say. "Everything's fine."

Sarah mutters, "You scared me."

Adam closes his eyes and screams, "Wake up!"

When he opens them again, Sarah is lowering herself back into the bed while the thing that isn't him kisses her forehead.

"Sarah!" He reaches for her, his arm moving with excruciating slowness. "Sarah, that's not me." His voice is made of molasses and the words are garbled and nonsensical.

Wake up… wake up… wake up…

Then he is yanked back into the room. He can see the Atlantic again, but only for a moment. It is soon consumed by an empty whiteness, as if it's being eaten by light.

"*No,*" Adam gasps. He says it in his mind now. His

mouth no longer works. The light begins to seep under the balcony door, flowing like ink from an overturned bottle.

What is this?

There's no reply. He screams as loudly as he can, *Where are you sending me?*

But he knows the answer. The dream thing at least gave him that much. And the answer isn't death. No, it's not as simple or merciful as that. It's something so much worse. The thing needs his body, but not his mind. So his mind will be locked away—destined to wander forever in the nothingness.

And as he feels himself begin to dissolve into the light, he realizes that he tried too hard to wake up this time.

THE SPAGHETTI INCIDENT

Lewis Williams

Amber stared in disbelief at the knife that Emily had just stuck in her stomach. It was as if all her thoughts needed to be occupied taking in this impossible information before she could even process the pain or the fact that her lifeblood was draining away. They had only been having an everyday row - nothing special, the kind of bickering they indulged in daily. The knife in her stomach didn't make any sense, but at the back of her mind she knew the real reason for it – something that happened many years ago, the spaghetti incident.

Although Amber and Emily were sisters, they couldn't have been more different. Emily was quiet and introverted; Amber was loud and boisterous. Where Emily had a small number of close friends, Amber was everybody's friend and everybody wanted to be Amber's friend. She was popular at school – one of the cool kids. Whereas Emily had spent every waking moment revising for her recent GCSEs, Amber adopted a cavalier attitude towards her exams, leaving any revision at all to the last minute and believing she could always get by with a mix of her innate intelligence, a late burst of effort and a little luck.

Her luck now, though, was running out, along with her blood – although, truth be told, it was the internal bleeding that was the more serious matter. As Amber felt herself slipping into unconsciousness, she kept telling herself, *it was years ago … it was years ago …*

Amber was nine. She'd persuaded her parents that she could cook the family a meal unaided. She knew how to use the oven and the hob and had done so with supervision quite a few times. Her parents were only in the next room and she'd shout if she had any problems at all. She wasn't going to do anything complicated, just her favourite, chicken nuggets, that she'd cook under the grill, oven chips, and Alphabetti Spaghetti that she'd heat in a saucepan on the hob.

So, with her parents' approval, she set to work. There really was nothing to it: pre-heat the oven, pre-heat the grill, then with the nuggets and chips cooking it was just a question of keeping an eye on turning them occasionally so they didn't burn and leaving five minutes at the end to heat up the Alphabetti Spaghetti. It required little skill. Her mind wandered to more creative endeavours.

Shortly, Amber carried the finished plates of food into the dining room, placing before her mum and dad each a perfectly cooked plate of chicken nuggets, Alphabetti Spaghetti and chips. But Emily's plate was special. Their parents tried to hide their amusement at it. They both tried and failed to keep a straight face, knowing that rather than be rewarded with their finding it funny, Amber deserved a serious telling off. Emily's plate had no chicken nuggets or chips, just twelve pieces of Alphabetti Spaghetti carefully arranged to spell out four words: EMILY IS A SHIT.

JOHN LONGMIRE'S LAST DAY

D.A. Watson

'Wake up, Mr Longmire.'

The voice calls me from sleep. I don't want to wake. Being awake hurts. For a few blessed seconds before my brain's fully conscious, there's nothing. Then comes the pain. That slow, creeping agony, radiating out from my core. I don't want to live with this pain anymore. That's why this will be my last day of my life. By this afternoon, I'll be dead. Blissfully, unfeelingly dead.

'Wake up,' says the voice again.

I open my eyes, and see a goddess.

I've known many beautiful women in my life. This one makes the others seem plain. For a moment, caught by the sight of her, I forget about the pain of my disintegrating insides, but even the sight of a goddess can't hold the hurt at bay for long, and it comes clawing insistently back. My body tenses. I groan through gritted teeth.

My afternoon cocktail of secobarbital and pentobarbital can't come quick enough.

'Here, let me,' the goddess says, reaching for the self-administering morphine pump at the side of my bed and giving the trigger a squeeze. She presses a cool soft hand to my brow, and the pain fades like a doused fire.

'Who are you?' I ask the goddess, my voice a grateful sigh as I relax back into the pillows. They're good pillows. Large, soft, with just the right balance of spring and give. Good pillows to lay your head on for an eternal sleep.

'Freja,' she says, gifting me a smile that would make Michelangelo weep. The bright early morning sunshine coming through my room's window behind her casts a glowing corona through her golden hair. That smile. Her eyes. A vivid blue flecked with violet. Intense and searching. She looks angelic. If I believed in God, or even an afterlife, I could almost believe I already died in my sleep and am looking upon one of the Almighty's seraphim.

'I'm here to talk about your options,' she says. She has a pleasantly lilting Nordic accent. One of the Mischler Clinic staff I assume, from the pristine white smock she wears and the clipboard in her hand.

I return her smile, the morphine starting to take hold. 'No options,' I say dreamily. 'Choice is made. Today, I go.' I close my eyes again, the morphine starting to flow sweet but temporary relief through my ruined innards.

'That is your choice, of course,' Freja says. 'But do you mind if I ask you a few questions nonetheless? It is standard procedure. Just a final check to ensure you are of completely sound mind, and have no lingering, possibly subconscious doubts about your decision.'

'Go ahead,' I mumble. Why not? I'm not going to change my mind, and her voice is very pleasant to listen to.

'Your full name?' she begins.

'John Graeme Longmire.'

'Birthday?'

'Eighth of February, nineteen-fifty-two.'

'Parents?'

'Harry and Kirsten Longmire.'

'Siblings?'

'None.'

'Spouse?'

'None. My third and most recent divorce was four years ago.'

'Do you have any children?' Freja asks.

'No. I never wanted any. Had a vasectomy when I was twenty-five.'

'Why?'

'I had a business to run, and when I wasn't working, I very much enjoyed the things the business brought me.'

'Such as?'

'Money. Cars. Women. Five-star hotels.' I shrug. 'Freedom. I didn't want to give any of it up for children.'

'Interesting,' Freja says. 'Some might say such a lifestyle might be... empty. Unfulfilling. Selfish even.'

'Selfish, certainly,' I agree. 'Empty and unfulfilling?' I fondly recall one particularly debauched evening in the company of a stunning five-grand-per-night escort, an uncut ounce of cocaine, a case of Cheval Blanc 1947 and a vibrating strap-on. 'Most assuredly not.'

Freja nods and makes a note on her clipboard, then fixes me with those wonderful eyes again. 'Your diagnosis?'

'Terminal colorectal, kidney and liver cancer.'

'Prognosis?'

'Dead in three months. Maybe four.'

'Why did you choose to be euthanised?'

I smile. 'Have you ever seen a final stage cancer patient?'

'Countless times,' Freja replies. 'You refused chemotherapy?'

'Yes.'

'Why?'

'I've lived long enough. Done everything I ever wanted to do. I have no interest in a few months of futile treatment, being so sick I can hardly move, never mind *enjoy* life, before dying anyway.'

'So you've chosen the easy way out?' she asks, and is that just a smidgen of disapproval in her voice?

'That's right,' I tell her, frowning and putting a little well-practised steel into my own words. 'That's what I'm paying you for.'

She's unflustered by my warning tone, though. Her smile actually widens a little. 'Oh, you're not paying me, Mr Longmire,' she says. She consults her clipboard. 'You are the CEO of Kestrel Technologies, yes?'

I sigh and close my eyes again. 'I am.' Let her ask her questions. What difference does it make?

'How old were you when you founded the company?'

'Twenty-two.'

'A young age to start your own business. Did you establish it on your own?'

'No. I had a partner.'

'Their name?'

'Ashton Scarrow.'

'How did you know Ashton?'

'We grew up together.' My eyes drift to the wide floor-to-ceiling window to the right of my bed. It affords a spectacular view out over a forest-fringed alpine lake, the same vivid icy blue as Freja's eyes. Beyond, the snow-capped peaks of the Swiss Alps extend all the way to the horizon.

'How would you describe your relationship with Ashton Scarrow?' Freja goes on.

I normally don't like talking about Ashton, but Freja's lulling voice, and the effect of the high-quality morphine, relaxes me, and I find I don't mind so much. 'He was my friend. I thought of him as my brother. Unlike me, Ashton came from a wealthy family. He put up the money to get us started. He was the creative one. The ideas man. I was the businessman. We made a good team.'

'Until his death,' Freja states.

I look over at her. 'Yes,' I say evenly. 'Until his death.'

'How did he die?'

That's pushing it. I give her a sour look. 'It was all over the media. I'd imagine you already know fine well how he died.'

'I do,' she says agreeably, 'but again, these questions are designed to gauge your psychological and emotional reactions. Please answer the question. How did Ashton Scarrow die?'

I let out a long sigh. 'He killed himself.'

'Why?'

'Oh for God's sake,' I say, patience running thin. 'Is this really necessary?'

'I understand some of these questions may seem a little… personal. Irrelevant, or inappropriate even,' she says apologetically. 'Please do not take offence. They are simply part of your final assessment, but we are almost finished. Why did Ashton Scarrow commit…'

'He was being blackmailed,' I interrupt, glaring at her. 'He had… certain appetites. Sexual appetites. Someone found out and threatened to expose him.'

Freja just stares back at me. 'He was a paedophile?'

'I'm sure you read his suicide note. That slimy little bastard groundskeeper who found him photographed it and sold it to the tabloids, as you well know. Now, are we done here?'

'Just a few more questions, I promise,' Freja says, softening her voice, that bewitching smile back on her face. I feel the anger draining out of me just looking at it. It's also hard to stay angry at someone when you have a few CCs of medical grade heroin pumping through you. 'Your company has appeared on the Global Fortune 500 list for the past twelve years?' Freja continues.

I close my eyes and relax back into my big comfy pillows. 'It has.'

'You are a very wealthy man, Mr Longmire.'

'I am.'

She pauses a beat before her next question. 'Would you say you are a *good* man?'

I open my eyes again and look over at her. Finally, we get to the point. 'Freja,' I say, 'as you just said, I'm a very wealthy man. That's the reason I'm here spending my last hours in the most respected, and costliest, euthanasia clinic in the world. It's the reason I was able to be here the day after my doctor gave me my test results. My point is, I'm not paying your organisation to check if I have some sort of repressed guilt complex. I'm paying the Mischler Clinic to *kill* me. I've done all the soul searching I intend to do, and I'm at peace with myself, and my decision to end my life. I'm not a religious man, and I don't believe in any afterlife judgement. I regret nothing. Not even my friendship with Ashton. I loved him. If that means I'm not a good man, then so be it. Now, lovely as you are to look at, I'm done with your questions. You have the order for my last meal?'

Freja consults her clipboard again. 'Yes. Salmon en croute and a bottle of Chateau Latour 2009.'

I nod and wave a hand dismissing her. 'Very good. Now, I have a strong urge to listen to my Sam Cooke playlist. Thanks for stopping by.' I find the iPod controller on the bed next to me and relax back into the luxuriant pillows, closing my eyes again. A moment later, the poignant sound of 'Bring It on Home to Me' fills the room, and I smile as Sam's unique croon caresses my ears, eliciting a pleasurable tingle on the skin of my forearms.

'Sam Cooke was murdered,' I hear Freja say.

'Yes, he was,' I whisper, not opening my eyes. 'Murder most foul. Poor Sam.'

'Just like Ashton Scarrow.'

My eyes snap open, and I find Freja leaning over the bed.

'It was not suicide,' she says, her voice cold as a knife in the dark. '*You* killed him.'

'What the fuck is this?' I demand, trying to sit up. 'I did *not* pay good money to…'

Freja places a hideously strong hand on my chest and pushes me back onto the mattress. The pain in my insides surges, and wracked with sudden agony, my vision washes red.

'Ashton's death paid good money too, did it not?'

Freja says. 'With him out the way, you were able to secure the contract with that electronics factory in Honduras.'

My mouth opens, but no words come out. The pain, and her accusations, make it too difficult to speak, or to think.

'He was a good man,' she continues. 'A moral man. When you went to his home that night and proposed what was effectively slave labour, he forbade it. You quarrelled, and when he turned his back on you in disgust, you strangled him with a red velvet curtain rope. *You* typed up his suicide note on his antique Remington typewriter. *You* dragged his body out to the grounds and hung him from the tree. And *you* planted those videos and images on his hard drive.'

No, it's not possible. How can she possibly…

'Thirty-seven people died in the first year in that factory in Honduras,' she says as she walks to the foot of the bed and looks down on me. 'Accidents. Exhaustion. Exposure to toxins. Some of them children. The youngest nine years old. But the low production cost enabled Kestrel to make its first million. That sweat shop contract was the rock on which the company's future success was built.'

Terrified, bewildered, I try to shake my head in denial, try to scream for help, but every agonised fibre in my body is locked in ice and fire.

She smiles at me then. 'You say you are not a religious man, Mr Longmire. You say you do not believe in an afterlife or judgement.' She gives me a pitying look, then leans forward over the foot of the bed, and holy Jesus, she appears to be… *glowing*. 'But you are wrong. *Everyone* is judged. *Everyone* must face a reckoning.'

I can't breathe. It feels like some ineffable part of me is being flayed to the bone by those terrible icy blue eyes. I try to avert my gaze from hers, because I'm certain that if I don't, I'll be burned to ash. But even my optical muscles are paralysed and I can't look away. The lights in the room dim and flicker, and it seems a freezing wind rises from nowhere.

'I told you I was here to talk about your options,' Freja goes on, 'so here they are. You can die today, be free of the pain of your cancer, and face what awaits you on the other side. Or you can live a few more months as your tumours consume you from within, and try to make reparation for the things you've done. As you said yourself, you are a wealthy man. That wealth could do much good in this world.'

That's when she rises off the floor, and glides forward till she hovers in the air directly over my prone body. I feel my mind start to fracture as her lovely face seems to melt like running tallow, the fine planes of her cheeks, that sensuous mouth, twisting and warping into something hideous, inhuman and ancient. Unable to move, unable to breathe or scream, I'm helpless as the wizened hag descends, that terrible puckered mouth opens to display crooked yellow fangs.

'*There must be a reckoning*,' Freja whispers, then starts to cackle as her jaw unhinges with an audible dry *crack*, and that hellish maw stretches impossibly wide, closing over my face…

Finally, I scream.

* * *

And wake up, thrashing in the sheets of my bed in the Mischler Clinic. I sit up gasping for air, heart slamming fit to burst my ribcage, and look frantically around the room.

I'm alone. Bright afternoon sunshine filters through the broad floor-to-ceiling window. No monstrous entity lurks in the corner. Like a frightened child, I lean over and look under the bed. Nothing there. I unhook the morphine pump from my arm and get out of bed, warily approaching the door to the private bathroom on very shaky legs. Steeling myself, I throw it open.

Nothing.

When the door to my room opens behind me, I let out a yelp of fright and spin around, expecting some wizened horror to come rushing at me, but it's only Dr Allaman, the physician who'll administer my lethal cocktail later today. He's looking at me strangely. Behind him comes a young dark-haired nurse pushing a trolley with a covered dish and a bottle of wine. My salmon and Chateau Latour.

'Are you alright, Mr Longmire?' the doctor asks in his pleasant, clipped voice.

For a second, I can't speak, and continue looking around the room warily. 'Yes,' I manage after a moment, my voice unsteady. 'I... I had a nightmare.'

Dr Allaman nods sympathetically. 'Quite normal, I assure you. A procedure such as yours commonly weighs heavy on the mind.' For the first time, I notice he's holding a clipboard. 'If you don't mind,' he says, taking a gold pen from his shirt pocket, 'it's standard procedure to ask you a few final questions before we go any further. Just to ensure you are absolutely certain of your choice and have no last-minute doubts.'

And I look at him silently, terror like cold lead filling me from the feet upwards.

THE BEST WEAPONS IN THE WORLD

Wondra Vanian

Veronica inherited many things from her mother. A love of yard sales was the one trait her husband, Shawn, most wished she hadn't. Nearly every Saturday during the summer was taken up by long car trips to unfamiliar towns, in search of nothing in particular so long as it was a "great find!" Luckily for Shawn, summer was drawing to a close and, with it, their weekend expeditions to yard sales far and wide.

September couldn't come fast enough.

Until then, there were dozens of yard sales in Shawn's future. As he steered the SUV onto a long, dusty driveway that led up to an old farmhouse, he found himself wondering absently if divorce would be cheaper than his wife's yard sale addiction.

Nothing stood out about that sale. Card tables stretched out across the overgrown lawn outside an ageing, two-story clapboard house. To Shawn's indifferent eye, they were filled with the same old junk he'd seen hundreds of times before. There was nothing special among the chipped dinner plates, threadbare jackets, or incomplete board games, as far as he could see.

But, then, he didn't have his wife's well-honed eye for trash.

"Ooh, look!" Veronica exclaimed excitedly as Shawn parked the car behind an old Cadillac. She was out the door before he'd even had a chance to turn the car off. With a defeated sigh (and barely repressing the urge to bang his head repeatedly against the steering wheel) Shawn followed his wife across the lawn toward the tables, resigned to the fact that most of it would probably be leaving in his trunk.

There was a time when Shawn would have tried to temper his wife's habit, arguing against buying fondue sets they didn't need (that *no one* had ever needed) and CDs they already had at home, but experience had taught him that there was no use. It would only end in a fight. The same one they'd been repeating for years. One he had yet to win.

He said nothing as Veronica made her way through the sale, digging through battered cardboard boxes, holding up articles of clothing that hadn't been fashionable in decades. Shawn shoved his hands in his pockets to keep from knocking the boxes over and dragging his wife away. Standing off to the side, he did his best to hide the scorn he felt behind a mask of boredom, waiting to be beckoned forward to carry something. (Or, more than likely, *several* somethings.)

"You have the look of a man who would rather be anywhere else," a gravelly voice said nearby, startling Shawn.

A woman who had to be seventy if a day sat in a folding chair in the shade of an even older tree. She had a book open in her lap, but her eyes were fixed on Shawn.

"Is it that obvious?" Shawn joked to cover his unease. Veronica could (and often *did*) talk a seller's ear off while perusing their rubbish, but he preferred to hang back to avoid awkward conversations.

Kind of like this one…

The old woman's gaze was steady and stronger than he would have thought possible at her advanced age. She was slight, dwarfed by the white plastic lounger she sat in, with skin like aged leather. Despite that, something about the woman made Shawn think she was what his mother would have called "a tough old broad."

His mother had never dragged anyone to a yard sale. She, rest her sensible soul, had known exactly where garbage belonged—and it wasn't crammed into the back of his SUV.

"Hey, Ma," a blonde woman a little older than Shawn called across the lawn. She stood next to Veronica, who held what looked *exactly* like the three crockpots they already had at home.

"How much is this?" the blonde called, holding up an earthenware casserole dish.

The old woman rolled her eyes. "I told you before, I don't care," she hollered back in a surprisingly loud voice. Surprisingly loud—and unmistakably annoyed.

"I didn't even want to have a yard sale," she confided to Shawn. "Hate the damned things."

Shawn leaned forward to say, conspiratorially, "Me too."

She chuckled, a husky sound, and nodded. "I'd guessed as much, my boy."

It had been a long time since anyone had called Shawn a "boy." He found he liked it.

The old woman gestured to a second, empty lounger. "If your wife there is anything like my husband, you might as well take a load off. My girl, Nancy, won't rest until she's sold her half the junk here."

Shawn hesitated only a moment before taking the offered seat. "Only half?" he joked.

He introduced himself and earned a "Marnie," in return.

"Nice to meet you, Marnie," he said and surprised himself by meaning it. The old woman nodded in return.

"And you, boy."

They watched Veronica and Nancy travel up a row of tables, chatting excitedly, for a few minutes. Eventually, Shawn broke the silence.

"I bet your husband wasn't happy about parting with this stuff," he said.

"Reggie's been gone, oh, must be at least twenty years," Marnie told him.

Open mouth, insert foot, Shawn thought.

"I'm so sorry," he said.

She waved away his condolences. "Don't be," she said. "It was me that killed him."

Shawn could only stare, open-mouthed, at the old woman.

"But," she said, "if the girl asks, he disappeared mysteriously." Air quotes and an exaggerated wink accompanied the final word.

Marnie gave him a look that suggested she was very amused by her little joke. Something about the deadpan way she admitted to offing her husband made Shawn wonder, though...

Don't be stupid, he told himself. *Look at her.*

She's barely big enough to kill a mouse.

Still, he had to appreciate her sense of humor.

…he thought.

He forced a laugh to cover the awkward silence. "I hope you didn't kill poor, old Reggie just because he didn't like yard sales!"

"Oh, no," Marnie assured him. "I killed Reggie because he hit me once too often, the bastard. Not having to go to another yard sale was just a bonus."

The women passed by, close enough to be within earshot, so Marnie lowered her voice. Leaning in close, she added, "You'd be surprised how easy it is to poison someone. Found a book on it at the library, I did."

Although he knew the old woman was joking, a quick shiver ran through Shawn. *Good lord,* he thought. *If that's what she can do with a library card, I hope no one ever teaches her to use the internet…*

"Look at all this fabulous stuff!" Veronica said, startling Shawn from his disturbing thoughts. She happily shoved a box that rattled with loose objects in his face. One corner was stained with a substance he didn't even want to try to identify.

He shoved the box away with a grimace. "Are you done?" he asked testily.

Veronica pouted at Shawn's lack of enthusiasm. "Yes," she said. "And, if we hurry, we can still make the sale over on Houston Road."

Shawn gave Marnie a sideways look as if to say, "See what I have to put up with?"

The old woman leaned in. "So, so easy…" she said with a wicked grin.

He didn't let himself imagine how easy life would be

without his wife in it. He didn't dare. If Shawn thought about it too long, he might find himself at the library, checking out books on poisonous plants.

"Ooh," Veronica said with an awed gasp, staring at a spot over Shawn's shoulder. "Look at *that!*"

Shawn half-turned in his chair to look in the direction his wife indicated. A ragged-looking scarecrow stood at the edge of an overgrown field—a twisted and grotesque thing in a faded duster and wide-brimmed hat that partially obscured its hideous face.

"It's stunning," Veronica breathed. "Where do you buy it?"

Marnie, who hadn't bothered looking, answered, "It's homemade."

Her daughter, Nancy, barely glanced at the scarecrow. "Awful, isn't it?" she said with a shiver. "Ma's had that thing forever," and turning to her mother asked her, "How long ago did you make that?"

"Oh," the old woman answered, absently waving a hand, "must be at least twenty years now." She still hadn't turned to look at the scarecrow.

Shawn's eyes grew wide as he looked from the scarecrow to Marnie, then back again. It was the right size and shape…

But Marnie didn't respond to his questioning gaze, her head down apparently having returned to her book.

"Is there…?" Veronica started. "Do you think maybe I could buy that too?"

"Ronnie!" Shawn exclaimed, as Marnie snapped back, "Absolutely not!"

Nancy gave her mother a disapproving look while Shawn shook his head vehemently.

"Why would you want something like that?" he demanded.

Veronica gave him a condescending look, as if it should be *obvious* what she had planned for it. "Just think of how great it would be for Halloween!"

"It's not for sale," Marnie reinforced in a tone that wasn't intended to allow room for argument. Her book had fallen to the ground, but she didn't seem to notice.

A couple who had only just stepped out of their car behind the SUV quietly climbed back in and drove away without approaching the loaded tables.

"Ma!" Nancy said, voice heavy with exasperation. "We've spoken about this. You can't take everything with you to the home."

Marnie's face was like thunder. "I'm not taking anything anywhere. *This* is my home."

Nancy sighed heavily and pinched the bridge of her nose between two fingers. "We'll talk about this later."

Judging by the look on her mother's face, it wasn't a conversation that was going to go well for Nancy. For her sake, he hoped none of the plants that grew on the farmland were lethal.

"We don't need a scarecrow," Shawn said, trying to reason with his wife. As if *that* had ever done any good. He was going to have as much luck arguing with her as Nancy was going to have arguing with her mother. At least he knew his wife had never stepped foot in a library...

And he'd survived five years of her cooking already, so he was pretty sure he was immune to poison.

Veronica rolled her eyes. "No one *needs* a scarecrow. It will look amazing, though. We can totally revamp the

Halloween decorations around it…"

The argument was by no means over but, by the time it was, neither Shawn nor Marnie came out on top. Money exchanged hands and Nancy started across the lawn to retrieve the scarecrow.

"No," Marnie snapped, "I'll do it."

She rose slowly, leaning heavily on the arm her daughter offered, then made her way to the scarecrow. The other women talked animatedly about Halloween, so they missed the way Marnie reached up to touch the scarecrow's face once before grabbing the post with both hands and pulling it from the ground.

It did not go easily. Marnie struggled with it until Nancy said, "Oh, Ma!" and hurried over to help.

"Well," Veronica said, obviously in a funk because Shawn had argued with her in front of other people, "are you going to open the trunk?"

Shawn couldn't look at the scarecrow as they loaded it into the trunk. Instead, he looked over to where Marnie stood. The old woman met his eye and shook her head. Sadly? It was hard to tell. He turned away as the trunk slammed shut and climbed into the driver's seat, resigned to taking the monstrosity home with him.

And her scarecrow.

* * *

Shawn did his best not to think about the creepy scarecrow lurking in a corner of the garage. It worked well enough until the first day of October, when Halloween fever struck his wife. By the time the sun set that day, the scarecrow had taken pride of place on his front lawn, far too near the front door for Shawn's taste. He had to pass the awful thing on his way in or out of the house. It chilled his blood every time his gaze fell on it.

"Would you get rid of that damned scarecrow?" he snapped one night as he removed his coat. After a long day at work, he was in no mood for his wife, her obsession with overdecorating for every holiday, or her stupid yard sale finds.

Veronica poked her head out of the kitchen to frown at him. "But we only just got it," she argued. She wore a frilled apron covered in frolicking kittens dressed as witches. He was certain it wasn't the same puppies-as-vampires one she wore the night before—and that she hadn't owned either of them when the week had started—but he didn't have the energy to start *that* fight.

"I don't like the scarecrow," he said. "It's… scary."

"It's *supposed* to be scary," Veronica countered with a chuckle. She didn't seem the least bit perturbed that the scarecrow upset her husband. If anything, she seemed quite pleased with herself. "Says so right in the name."

Shawn couldn't make any argument that would change his wife's mind. And he tried them all. At one point, he shouted that it was either him or the scarecrow and stormed out the door—but not before she answered with, "The scarecrow is better looking, anyway."

Engine revving, Shawn swung the SUV out of the driveway and sped away into the night. He wasn't sure exactly where he was going, only that he wanted to be very, very far away from his wife and the secondhand scarecrow she refused to part with. Even though he didn't have a destination in mind, Shawn wasn't all that surprised when he found himself back at the old farmhouse where the yard sale was held months ago.

He sat in the dark, trying to cool his temper. It took a long time. After a while, Shawn realized that he'd been staring at the same spot for some time without really seeing it. When he focused on it, he recoiled, heart thumping heavily in his chest.

A scarecrow.

There was a scarecrow at the edge of the field behind the farmhouse.

Can't escape the damned thing…

Curiosity got the better of Shawn. He drove up the long drive, parked, and got out without turning off the car. The SUV's headlights fell across the new scarecrow. Shawn walked up to it slowly, taking in the little details highlighted by the car's lights.

It was different from the original scarecrow in that it was smaller and shorter. Although encased in a bulky sweater stuffed with straw, the shape was obviously female. The scarecrow had a mop of matted blonde hair tucked under a knitted hat. It wasn't as shriveled or weather-worn as the first scarecrow. In fact, Shawn thought he could almost make out features…

He jumped when a porchlight flared to life. A door swung open with a creak.

"Well," a familiar gravelly voice called, "you might as well come in. I'll put a pot of coffee on."

Marnie stood haloed in the open doorway. Shawn looked from her to the scarecrow, came to some very disturbing conclusions very quickly, and joined her anyway.

"Hello again, boy," the old woman said as Shawn settled himself at the small wooden table in her kitchen.

"I wondered when you'd be back."

Shawn looked around. The kitchen looked well lived in but not cluttered. There weren't any signs of things being packed up for a move.

"I thought you were going to a home," he said, taking the steaming cup she offered.

Marnie gave a snort of derision. "Over my dead body."

Shawn cleared his throat. "Or… your daughter's?"

The old woman raised her eyebrows but said nothing. The corners of her mouth *definitely* quirked up as she lifted the cup to her lips, though.

Suspicions more or less confirmed, Shawn found he wasn't as disturbed by the thought as he probably should have been. He thought he knew the reason for that but wasn't ready to admit it to himself.

He wondered if it was safe to drink the coffee she'd offered. Marnie just raised her eyebrows in silent challenge until Shawn took a tentative sip. If it was poisoned, it was tasty. The old woman laughed out loud.

She set her cup down on the table and pushed herself to her feet. "Glad you're here. I've got something for you, boy," she told him. Then she disappeared into the hallway and, after a few minutes, came back with a book in her hand.

"Suppose you might be needing this," she said, laying the book on the table in front of Shawn. It was wrapped in a plastic dustjacket, with a label on the spine that bore a Dewy Decimal number and the word "reference." The cover showed only two things, a golden sarcophagus and the title.

Mummification and Egyptian Death Practices.

Marnie went to refill the coffee pot as Shawn opened the book and began to read. "Mind you return that on time," she warned. "I just started reading a book about the Salem witch trials and I don't like late-fees."

She laughed then, and Shawn decided that she was probably joking. He'd mark his calendar, though, just in case...

PARADISE MODIFIED

Cathy Bryant

Steve had done it without my knowledge or permission, and I was furious. I rattled dishes unnecessarily, and glared at him until he got the point.

'Anne, darling,' he said in an incredibly irritating tone of voice, no doubt supposed to soothe me. 'That tree has canker. It'll have to come down and be burned at some point anyway, eventually.'

'*Eventually*, yes,' I snapped. 'But that tree has grown for over a hundred years without any pesticides or other nonsense. And cankered trees can live for ages and continue to produce edible fruit. I've been eating apples from that tree ever since I was weaned, and now I won't dare to. What genetically modified rubbish have you poisoned it with?'

Like the smug biochemist he was, Steve came out with one of those scientific words that take ten syllables to convey nothing whatsoever. I very nearly smashed a cup as I was putting it away, but noticed at the last minute that it was my favourite and placed it carefully down; as for Steve, I made do with scowling at him severely.

After a bit more rowing and some time later, we made up. Steve promised 'to try to remember' to consult me about household decisions that would affect me, and I said that I'd try not to get so angry with him.

Living in the country was hard for Steve. I'd been born to the valley, and loved the peace and the constantly changing face of Nature, but he'd had to adjust to the isolation and the long commute to his lab.

That night, however, listening to his snoring, my resentment welled up again. The tree's branches tapped against the bedroom window as if asking me for help, or admonishing me for failing to provide it. I hoped that the robins nesting in it would be OK, and their four eggs – tiny, buff, speckled treasures.

'I'm sorry,' I whispered, sleepless. Steve continued to snore as evenly and regularly as a car alarm, and as annoyingly. But I loved him, and snuggled up to him to get some warmth and comfort at least, if not much sleep. I dozed off just as it was getting light, to the sound of the wind hissing in the trees.

Over the next week I kept staring at the apple tree. There was a livid yellow patch where Steve had injected it, and instead of fading it was swelling, winding round the trunk. It was a grotesque shape, vaguely phallic.

I didn't say anything, though - it wasn't until the robin incident that I argued with Steve again.

On a sultry still day I looked out and saw that the nest had gone.

I fumed all day and laid into him the second he got home.

'So, what was the problem with the nest then?' I asked. 'Did it have canker too?'

He frowned. 'What? What nest?'

'The robins. You knocked it down, didn't you? Was it while I was at the shops? Did you kill the birds or are they going to die a slow homeless death?'

'Anne, I didn't do a damn thing to any nest. Stop accusing me!'

'I suppose it just disappeared.'

'It probably fell. They sometimes do.'

'There's no sign of it. And there hasn't been a breath of wind.'

Steve looked at me coldly and walked out of the house.

Then I heard him say, 'That's weird.' He'd said it to himself, but I just caught it.

'What?' I said, joining him. '– Oh!'

The tree had a growth - a bulge about the size of a side plate. It was bulbous and matty-looking but mossed over, as if it had been there for years. And there were small bulges at the sides, shaped like – shaped like bir—

My head knew straight away what it was, but I rejected the knowledge. There are things our minds won't accept, so that we can stay sane.

'Is it – canker?' I asked hopefully, knowing that it wasn't.

'No. Canker can't do that,' Steve said shortly, and reached up to the growth.

'No!' I grabbed his hand before it could touch the – tree. I tried to laugh it off. 'Curiosity killed the – the—'

Both our hands were shaking.

I tried to put my thoughts into words. 'Could the nest and the two birds have fallen inside the trunk, and be pushing the bark out from the inside?'

Steve told me not to be ridiculous.

Back in the house we were silent for a while. The sight of the 'growth' had knocked the force out of our argument. Then Steve said cheerfully, 'It probably is canker, you know,' and I saw that he had put it out of his mind. That frightened me as much as anything, and made me feel very alone.

In the night the wind made a great hissing in the tree. I got up to look at it and caught my breath as I saw the branches writhing and twisting. Some were dark and slimy, some a bilious yellow, and some had patterns like little tombstones. The hissing noise came from the mouths at the end of the branches, and the little ones at the end of the twigs, where wormy horrors wriggled. It was obscene. I looked away across the valley – not one of the other trees was moving; there was no sound of wind apart from the thrashing of our apple tree. I hoped that I was dreaming and would soon wake up, but the sights and sounds suggested otherwise. It was all too vivid and immediate. And to think that I had felt hot and wanted to open the window.

It knocked the pane more loudly than usual.

'You can't come in,' I whispered.

It knocked again, harder.

'Whassat?' muttered Steve, blearing into consciousness.

'The tree on the window pane as usual. Go back to sleep.'

He tried, I think, but the noise was invasive and penetrating. He slippered over to the window.

'Bloody hell!'

We stared at the twisted mass as it flailed and wrenched, grasping angrily.

'So, what the hell was that stuff you put in – and don't just say the long word again.'

'It was from the lab. It's derived from snakes.'

I nodded. I'd known, really.

'I'm going to cut that bastard down now,' said Steve, pulling on his dressing gown.

'No!'

'Anne, look at it!'

'I know, but it'll kill you!'

'No it won't, because I'll have a damn great axe,' he said, and stomped downstairs.

'Please – please don't,' I begged, following him. 'Not at *night,* anyway.'

He just gave me a look, and got out the axe from under the sink. It looked reassuringly primitive – a lump of wood and a lump of metal, attached to each other – but I knew that it wasn't enough.

'Don't go, don't go,' I said hopelessly, my hands over my face as he opened the door and left.

There was one almighty THUK of axe on tree.

And then there was nothing.

I waited.

Perhaps Steve had dropped the axe or hurt himself, and needed my help. I forced my feet to walk to the door, and my hand to open it a crack.

The axe lay on the ground; there was no blood on it. I couldn't make myself look directly at the tree, but I could make out enough of the hunched misshapen trunk, branches massed and writhing like maggots in a bait tin, from the periphery of my vision. I slammed the door closed and breathed in and out, great gulping breaths.

My first thought was the phone, but just who do you

call to explain that your husband has been eaten by a were-snake tree? I laughed loudly at that and couldn't stop.

I couldn't explain it to anyone, and there was nothing I could do. My hysterical, horrible laughter rang round the house, but it was better than the hissing of the tree. In the morning I would go away, find someone and do something – I didn't know what. The tree would have to be destroyed, of course. What if it blossomed – and then fruited? What if innocent children came and reached up to pluck the apples – to bite into them – and if they survived long enough, instead of finding a harmless worm inside there would be a deadly— what if they swallowed—?

Like a child I headed instinctively for bed, to hide under the covers.

That's where I am now.

I sat here and wrote this. I wonder if it'll survive what's coming.

The branches are pounding on the window pane in a slow, relentless rhythm. The sound reminds me of the fatal cough of cannon, seen in old films. Or jungle drums, ditto.

I don't think I'll have to worry about anything in the morning. The glass will break soon, and the branches will find a way to reach me (the tree has grown, oh it has grown so big!) where I lie sobbing under the bedclothes, longing passionately for the prosaic bliss, the intimacy and innocence, of just one more flaming row with Steve.

THE FINAL STRAW

Sue Eaton

'There's too much flesh,' I mutter as I stand back and survey my handiwork.

'You should have thought of that,' my husband tells me in that 'I told you so' manner he has and I have grown to loathe over the years. 'If you'd have thought things through properly you would have taken that into account.'

'Yet who would have thought the old man to have had so much blood in him?' I moan as I watch the sticky red essence pool across the tiled floor, running through the channels of grout between tiles. I am suddenly aware that the underfloor heating is on. He always puts the underfloor heating on, however warm the day. It annoys the crap out of me, and it will dry up the blood if I don't get a shift on and finish cleaning up.

'Show off. You always thought you were so much better than me.'

'Never,' I correct him as I study the body before me.

'At least I know you're quoting Lady Macbeth – which, if you ask me, I find very apt."

'You can shut up. Shut up!' I stamp my foot, but the warm sticky blood under my trainer reduces the effect I had hoped for. 'If you'd shut up in the first place, I wouldn't be in this mess,' I tell him. Tears are starting to run silently down through the blood splatters on my face.

'You're in a mess? What about me? At least your mess will come out in the wash, which is more than can be said for me.'

'Not if I'm caught,' I tell him and sigh. 'O that this too too solid flesh would melt.'

'Good God! Am I to become a Shakespearian tragedy?' he snarls. 'That would just suit you, wouldn't it?'

'As you won't melt, I suppose I'll have to cut you up. You won't fit in the freezer in this state.'

'If it was up to me, I wouldn't choose to go in the freezer in any state,' hubby whines.

I leave my husband lying on the floor of the blood-splattered wet room and go in search of some sort of blade. The one I stabbed him with isn't strong enough for sawing through bone and sinew. It was an impulse thing; the final straw and I had just grabbed the nearest thing to hand, which happened to be a kitchen knife he'd left lying around after cutting the packaging from some purchase or another. I find nothing suitable.

'Where have you left the electric saw, you miserable old bastard?' I weep.

'As if I'd tell you,' he sniggers. 'You'd only saw me up for dog food if I did.'

'You never put anything away. You just leave your stuff lying around, forget where you put it then waste money we haven't got buying new. You don't even bother to look for them. The freezer's too good for you.' I am crying openly now.

'"You should have put your tools ready before you started the job,"' he quotes me at me in a put-on whiney voice and sniggers. 'Isn't that what you're always telling me?'

That really makes me see red. The claw hammer is to hand so I smack it into his mouth to stop the prattle. I suppose the police will wonder why I keep a hammer in a wet room – *I* wonder why there's a hammer in the wet room, but then I smack it into his eyes so he can't see what I'm doing. I just hammer away at him because he has annoyed me so much. I hammer away until I feel all my frustrations leak over the floor and mingle with the blood drying on the tiles. I hammer away until I am exhausted and empty, and slide down to the floor shaking and crying.

The sound of the doorbell ringing startles me, and I survey the mess. I can't speak to anyone looking like this. My T-shirt is soaked in blood and brain, and my jeans are sticking to my legs, and both are stiffening as it dries, so I get to my feet and turn on the shower. I have to step over the body to get underneath the flow, but it's not really in my way, not anymore.

I strip off my clothes as I stand under the shower and leave them in a heap on the floor. I stretch my limbs in the warm cascade, and idly watch the bloody water flow from my body and swirl down the drain. I stand until the water runs clear and then soap bits of my infuriating husband from my hair and skin.

The doorbell has long stopped its ringing by the time I am washed, dry and dressed ready to greet whoever was there. I don't care. It's so quiet. It's too quiet. I venture back into the wet room and study the scene.

It's a hot day, thundery and heavy, and flies have already wriggled in through the open vents and are swarming over the body, some paddling in the blood. They buzz and flit and annoy me nearly as much as he did.

'Say something then,' I demand, but the body stays silent this time. I kick him in his ample belly. The flies swarm angrily into the air only to settle again as soon as I stop. 'Say something now, you bastard!' I kick him again for good measure, but I'm tiring and the flies are bothering me.

'Ask me again where I've hidden your bloody car keys.' I start to sob and find I can't stop. I have to leave the house; I can't stand the smell or the incessant buzzing any longer. I leave the flies to their feast, shutting the wet room door quietly so as not to disturb them, and take the car keys from their usual place on the key hook by the back door.

I don't care where I go as long as it's not in this house. I don't care what will happen when he is found. I don't care about anything anymore.

FOOLISH PURSUIT

Suzanne Ross Jones

When Dawn first met Douglas it was obsession at first sight. At least on her part.

From the top of his expertly styled hair to the toes of his gleaming shoes, he was a perfect specimen of male beauty.

Dawn adored anything beautiful – that was why she spent so much time gazing at her own reflection.

'And this is Dawn,' Tania, the colleague who had persuaded her along for a drink after work, completed the introduction.

Dawn smiled, her heartbeat accelerating in anticipation of the moment when he would reach out and take her outstretched hand.

But he didn't.

He nodded in brief acknowledgement and instantly turned away to scan the crowded pub.

In someone less gorgeous, this behaviour would have been impossibly rude, but with Douglas it made him more attractive.

Silent, dark and brooding.

Dawn was intrigued.

'Can I buy you a drink?' she asked with a look that would have melted a lesser man.

'No thanks,' he mumbled without even glancing her way.

Without another word, he downed his drink in one and headed for the door.

Dawn stared after him, imagining how it might have been.

'Forget it,' Tania advised. 'He's getting over a doomed love affair. Swears he's not going to get involved with anyone else. You'd need Old Eliza to concoct some kind of love potion to get him interested.'

Dawn knew who Old Eliza was. Everybody did. She was the one who they said was a witch, who lived in the woods. Dawn shuddered at the thought.

But Douglas was a challenge Dawn couldn't resist. And she was sure she could succeed without any supernatural help. 'What happened? Why was the affair doomed?'

'She left him for his best friend.'

A crazy woman, Dawn decided. She would have to be to have left Douglas.

Never mind. Dawn would console him. A couple of hours in her company and he'd forget the other woman had ever existed.

Douglas, however, didn't want to forget. Dawn eventually got to buy Douglas that drink two evenings later and was rewarded by him telling her, in excruciating detail, about his affair with Cara. By the time she had heard the story a second time she was ready to scream.

A less determined woman would have given up. But not Dawn. She was proud of the fact that no man had ever been able to resist her, and she was adamant Douglas would not be the first.

It was a matter of pride. When you were as beautiful as she was you had a certain standard to maintain. You couldn't be seen to be losing your touch or people would start to laugh.

It wasn't even about Douglas any longer. In fact, if she was honest, his conversations were a bit tedious. He didn't even bore her with football like normal blokes: his sole topic of conversation was his lost love, Cara.

'Why don't you just give up?' Tania asked wearily. 'He's not worth it.'

'Perhaps not,' Dawn replied. 'But I'm not giving in now. I've invested too much time and energy.'

'The words dead horse and flogging come to mind,' Tania muttered, but Dawn was too preoccupied to notice.

What was that Tania had suggested that first night? Dawn did her best to remember. Getting Old Eliza to help, that was it.

Well, why not? She'd already tried almost everything else. She had nothing to lose by consulting the old woman. And, who knew, if the rumour-mongers were right she might have everything to gain.

By the time she arrived at Old Eliza's cottage she wished she hadn't bothered. From the road, it had been a half an hour trek through thick forest. Her tights were ripped, she'd broken three nails and her favourite shoes were scratched to a point where they were beyond salvation.

To top it all, Eliza wasn't answering the door. Dawn gave one last frantic thump before barging straight in.

It took a while for her eyes to become accustomed to the gloom, but when they did she squirmed. Cobwebs of magnificent proportions adorned the ceiling, and heaven alone knew how many layers of filth covered the floor.

This was all a complete waste of time, Dawn realised. Surely anyone with the kinds of powers Old Eliza was meant to have would use their abilities to get the housework done.

And it wasn't just the cottage that needed a major revamp. Eliza was sitting quietly in a corner and the sight of the woman made Dawn shudder. She was everything Dawn feared – she was wrinkled and very, very ancient. Some said that Eliza was more than three hundred years old. Looking at her now Dawn could well believe it.

The piercing blue eyes were the one redeeming feature in that withered old face – eyes that gave the impression that the old woman missed nothing.

And then she smiled, and the warmth of that smile reached out to Dawn and gave her hope.

She came straight to the point. 'I've heard you're a witch.'

The old woman seemed momentarily confused and Dawn realised she'd made an unforgivable mistake. This was just a harmless, elderly woman.

'Look, I'm sorry to have troubled you,' she mumbled, turning towards the door.

'Please, sit,' the words reverberated through the cottage – spinning in Dawn's head until she could do nothing but comply.

Old Eliza watched her for several unnerving minutes.

'What do you want?' she eventually asked.

'Your help. They say you can make love potions…'

'A man.' Eliza nodded as though she had seen it all before.

'Yes, a man. His name's Douglas. He's the most…'

Eliza raised a leathered hand. 'I don't need to know, dear.'

'I need him to fall in love with me,' Dawn continued. 'I can pay you.' At that Dawn opened her handbag and removed a handful of banknotes. Thank goodness she'd thought to go to the cash machine.

Old Eliza glanced at the banknotes and snorted. 'I don't need your money.'

'So you won't help me?'

'I didn't say that.'

Dawn sighed. 'I won't be ignored,' she said. 'He has to adore me. I'll settle for nothing less.'

'And what are you prepared to give to make this happen?'

Dawn looked at her money, confused. 'I thought you said you didn't want to be paid.'

'I don't need money,' Eliza said. 'But I will need payment.'

Dawn was confused but didn't ask questions.

'Go back to your life,' the old woman commanded. 'When you get there this man will find you irresistible, will want to be with you forever.'

It was all that Dawn had wanted when she had arrived at this cottage. Now all she wanted was to go home. 'Er, thanks. And what about your payment?'

'Don't worry about that. I'll take that when the time's right.'

With that cryptic statement ringing in her ears, Dawn made her way home. And there was a surprise waiting for her – Douglas in all his manly beauty was leaning against her front door. His smile made her want to swoon.

'I've been waiting for you,' he murmured seductively.

It had worked. Dawn hadn't really expected that it would, but Douglas was here, gazing longingly at her.

Magically, all stories of Cara had vanished from his conversation. Now all he spoke of was Dawn. How beautiful she was. How much he loved her. How he would die for her.

He wasn't so much of a bore any longer. Dawn began to think that there might be a future for them after all.

A gorgeous man who adored her above all else. What more could any woman want?

Dawn realised exactly what more the next morning.

She sat at her dressing table in preparation for adorning herself with creams and powders. As she raised the hairbrush her vision blurred.

Suddenly she wasn't staring at her own reflection any longer. A piercing scream escaped her.

Douglas was immediately at her side. 'Darling, what's the matter?'

'My face,' Dawn gasped with horror. 'My hair. Look.'

'Yes, darling. I am looking. You're beautiful.' Blinded by love. Douglas still found her irresistible.

Dawn raised a leathered hand to touch her wrinkled face. Her glossy, long hair had turned sparse and white. Instead of her own smooth, clear skin and perfectly proportioned features, the deeply wrinkled face of Old Eliza stared back at her.

* * *

Deep in the forest, Eliza brushed her glossy, long hair and admired her smooth, clear skin and perfectly proportioned features.

There was always one every century, she mused, grateful for Dawn's foolish pursuit of her man.

THINK BETTER OF IT

C.C. Adams

The wise man in the storm prays to God, not for safety from danger, but for deliverance from fear. It is the storm within that endangers him, not the storm without.

Ralph Waldo Emerson

Six-foot-one and two hundred and fifty-eight pounds of fat-clad muscle in a sleeveless T-shirt and shorts, Vernon sighed as he stepped out onto the balcony and the damp cool of the fresh evening air hit him – dusk and rain falling over South London. He folded his arms and rested his elbows on the thick and cold concrete of the ledge. Rain spanned his field of vision, spattering the street and its slow-rolling traffic below him. The old houses across the street stood wetly lacquered by the rain – a dull and stately uniformity of crumbling brickwork and dirty windows: some revealing the flickering light of a TV or an occupant moving from room to room. Vernon's own front door stood half-open behind him to his left side. To his right, along the balcony, the door of the neighbouring flat remained shut. He hardly needed to look to know that there would be no light behind the high window in the door. The couple were rarely home.

Whatever job they did, Vernon mused, allowed them a good life. He couldn't recall when exactly he'd last seen them wheeling their luggage in or out of the flat, but he knew it had been sometime within the last month. More importantly, the couple had looked – and *acted* – like a genuine team: the man confident and amiable with an easy athleticism about him, the woman no less friendly but exuding a quiet and obvious affection for her beau, never missing a chance to squeeze his hand or plant a loving kiss on his cheek.

Vernon swallowed hard and turned his glance away from the door, mentally holding the memory at arm's length. The woman was tactile and thoughtful: not a polar opposite to Julia, maybe, but they were as different as chalk and cheese. Julia had told him she felt stifled in the relationship, needed some space and that a temporary separation was for the best. Forever laidback, Vernon had agreed that she should do what she thought was best for her, but even before she had collected the last of her cosmetics from his flat, he was telling himself that she was full of shit. Whatever (or whoever) she was doing now, he was sure she wouldn't be spending too much time dwelling on thoughts of him.

In the short time he'd been standing on the balcony, the rain had intensified and now began to sheet in front of him. He inhaled. The rainclouds overhead had lowered the temperature of what had been a spring-like mid-April day in the city. The air he breathed in was cool but hardly fresh, polluted as it was by the volumes of exhaust fumes from the street below, where vehicles crawled obediently as dictated by traffic lights. The grass of the park-cum-play area yards from his block of flats sat bordered by cold hard tarmac, which shone black and wetly under the clouds' assault. In spite of himself, Vernon smiled. He had only come outside for a cigarette, which he had yet to light, but found himself strangely captivated by the view he had of Earlsfield on this rainy evening – in which he could detect something like a melancholy beauty. His cold that had been bothering him for the past few days was finally clearing up, and he counted himself lucky that he didn't get hay fever like some people. Lucas would get it the worst, with red-rimmed eyes weeping as if they were sprayed with lemon juice. For all the times the two of them supervised the door, he'd slap the bitch that dared to crack jokes about Lucas being a cry-baby.

Vernon craned his neck to look straight down from the top floor of the apartment block to the ground directly below, the tarmac path. A building from the 1970s, the block held a mere nine flats with three on each floor, all accessible from the draughty brick stairwell. Nevertheless, each flat provided a comfortable, well-furnished three-bedroom living space with a kitchen and bathroom – all at an agreeable price. Spacious, it was. Without Julia, a home it wasn't. Not anymore.

A gust of wind blew rain across his cheek and he turned away from it, squinting, and noticing two boys down below at the edge of the park. His gaze settled on them. He pegged the older taller boy at early teens, the younger one at about eight or nine years of age. Nothing remarkable in their appearance: the older boy wore a zipped-up jacket, jeans and trainers; the younger boy a dark sweatshirt, pale blue jeans and dark shoes. What caught Vernon's attention was the body language of the two. The younger boy stood with his hands clasped before his crotch and his head bowed; the older boy stood facing him, gesticulating sharply. As a bouncer, long before the phrase 'door supervisor' gained popularity, Vernon had learned to recognise the early signs of trouble and altercations from body language.

He strained to see if he could hear what was being said, but no shouts or snatches of conversation drifted back from the two boys. All he could hear was the rain and wind rustling the trees that stood sentry at generous intervals along the pavement and outside the apartment block. The larger boy stepped directly in front of the other and poked a finger in his chest. No reaction. Then the bigger boy brought both hands up to his opponent's chest and shoved, sending the younger boy sprawling backward.

Vernon gripped the balcony and craned his neck at the scene. 'Hey!'

The older boy looked up, his expression inscrutable. Turning back to his felled opponent, he stooped with his hands on his knees as if to follow his violence with a threat or parting shot before walking away. As he left the scene, Vernon noticed the boy palming the rainwater away from his face by running his hands back over his scalp. The younger boy sat where he lay after the shove.

And then he looked up.

Vernon felt a chill skim over him and goosebumps rose on his exposed flesh. His sandaled feet fidgeted in the gloom of the balcony floor.

The boy clambered to his feet, dusting himself off with all the slow deliberation of a pensioner stroking a pampered pet. Seeing the younger boy hadn't come to any real physical harm, Vernon offered himself a congratulatory all's-well-that-ends-well shrug …but paused when he saw the boy take the path that led into his apartment block. Vernon wasn't really in the mood for company but pursed his lips in rueful resignation. *Maybe it's just to show a little gratitude*, he thought. *Nothing wrong with gratitude, it shows some manners. Shows some class.*

Footsteps, light and quick, sounded at the bottom of the stairwell, growing louder and clearer as they drew near. Vernon turned to face the stairwell, leaning back on the balcony, with his arms folded and the wind blowing at his back.

The boy shuffled into view, his head bowed as if expecting a scolding, his hands clasped at his crotch. Vernon found the boy's demeanour misplaced: too formal. 'How you doing, fella?' Vernon said, offering a smile he hoped looked open and easy-going.

The boy began to sway a little, as if fidgeting would speak for him. His lips trembled. 'I'm okay,' he said eventually, his voice a light and feathery whisper.

'Good. I'm glad things are in hand. No one needs the drama, let alone in weather like this,' Vernon said, jerking his head to the sheeting rain behind him. 'Where were you heading?'

'May I use your phone?'

Vernon was taken aback. He frowned and folded his arms a little tighter. The boy hadn't even answered his question before assuming Vernon would want to lend him his phone.

'Who're you gonna call?' As soon as the words left his mouth, he bit his lip with a rueful smile, mentally pushing the Ghostbusters logo away. No matter how valid, you just couldn't use that phrase again without the same reference coming to mind.

The boy's head dipped as the wind ruffled his jet-black hair. 'I want to call my mother so that she doesn't worry about me. If I can let her know that I'm safe, then I can be on my way. May I call her?'

The boy's manner was strange. Various scenarios crossed Vernon's mind within moments: the boy was the victim of abuse in the home and needed a little coaxing to reveal the full story; the boy was up to no good and simply an opportunistic thief; the boy had a sense of misplaced bravado and was looking to prove himself.

But?

Vernon heaved a sigh.

Perhaps the boy had autism. Not that Vernon knew much about it, apart from autistic people might be lacking in social skills and awareness. That would explain the altercation he saw; kids could really be malicious little bastards when they put their mind to it. But, on the *other* hand?

Maybe the whole thing was a bait and switch; the altercation staged for his benefit. Not only malicious, but kids could be conniving little bastards. No shopkeeper in their right mind would let kids into their shop without enforcing the likes of the two-at-a-time rule.

No. *That* wasn't it.

Surely not.

He was being too suspicious. *Just because you feel hard done by Julia, you're gonna pay that forward? What kind of man does that make you?*

Still, not once had the kid made eye contact. Of

course, there could be a number of reasons for it …but *something* didn't fit. For the life of him, Vernon couldn't put his finger on it, but it was *there*.

Tall enough to look over the boy's head, Vernon trained his gaze on the stairwell. No movement, no shadow, no scuffing of footsteps on stone stairs (and in that musty and cobwebbed stairwell, the acoustics were great).

It's only him.

What's he gonna do, rob you all by himself? He can't even look you in the eye.

'Sure, after you,' Vernon said eventually.

The boy gave a brief nod and went in, his hands still clasped in front of his crotch. As he walked past, Vernon noted a slight curve to the corner of the boy's mouth …a disquieting smile.

Vernon felt the skin on his scrotum crawl and tighten.

He watched as the boy made his way inside. His overall posture didn't change; the boy didn't glance up, look ahead, crane his neck; no. None of those things. Vernon slid his tongue into his cheek, pensive, as he weighed up his guest. The boy's clothing looked damp, his hair tousled, but certainly not the bedraggled look Vernon would have expected. As the boy disappeared from view, Vernon pushed himself away from the wall and went back into the flat. He found the boy had already made his way into the lounge. On the TV in the near corner, a repeat of *Who Wants to Be a Millionaire?* saw Chris Tarrant asking a contestant if he was giving his final answer. The boy's attention was held, not by the TV, but the far wall. Two battered armchairs sat at awkward angles on either side of a mantelpiece adorned with framed pictures of various sizes while a snow globe sat in the middle. The plain bowl lampshade from the overhead light in the ceiling threw an ochre-yellow light over the room. Standing directly behind the boy and not able to follow his gaze, Vernon inhaled, just loud enough to catch the boy's attention. 'Which one's got your attention?'

The boy cocked his head, almost doglike. 'I like her. I can see why you like her.'

Julia. 'Yeah, well, that's all over and done with now. Of course, I could tell you that with women, you can't live with them and can't live without them, but you'll probably find that out for yourself one day.'

Applause sounded from the TV as the contestant was congratulated for a good effort as he made his way back to his fellow contestants.

If he was being honest with himself, Vernon was feeling a growing desire to be left in peace, to be left in solitude without this strange boy to deal with, in blissful ignorance of whatever the deal was with him. Never mind the fact that he never did have the cigarette that he actually –

'You look nervous,' the boy said suddenly.

Vernon paused.

The boy still had his back to him.

What?!

A twang of fear pricked his insides like hot needles. On the heels of that, a faint sense of nausea coasted through him like a fog.

'Wh-what did you say?'

The boy's shoulders lifted and fell in a shrug. 'You heard me. Or would you like me to repeat myself?'

Vernon's tongue felt riveted to the floor of his mouth. Attempts to swallow yielded nothing but awkward clicks from the back of his throat, his mouth feeling dry of saliva.

'I apologise. I asked to use your phone and you graciously invited me into your home. The least I can do is be quick.' The voice was still that of a child but with none of the attitude or *persona* of a child.

Vernon reached for his mobile phone, that was sitting on the dinner table next to him by the door of the lounge. Although fighting to stay calm, his trembling fingers nearly knocked the phone onto the floor. A desperate grab and he managed to trap it against the side of the table under one finger, the abrupt motion lighting up the phone's keypad. Leaning forward, he carefully wrapped his fingers around the handset, clutching the phone tightly. As his fingers tightened, he began to feel a pressing sensation upon his chest, as though a weight getting progressively heavier were crushing him. He steadied himself against the table. On the TV screen, another contestant pondered her next answer while tension music played.

The boy turned around, and Vernon could see a frown on the young face. As the boy came closer, Vernon tensed yet more. Something about the boy's face – or expression – seemed lifeless. Long moments stretched by as Vernon tried to figure out the source of the unease …until his gaze settled on the boy's unblinking eyes. The expression itself held no more humanity than a shop-window mannequin, but the eyes? Black: from corner to corner, lid to lid.

No whites.

No irises.

No pupils.

Now, from less than a few yards away, Vernon could smell the boy: the damp of his clothes, the wetness of his hair and skin, and a smell he could only describe as earthy, as though the boy had rolled around in moist earth … or crawled out of it.

'I thought I asked you to give me the phone.' The boy's eyes widened, revealing more of the same obsidian black.

Vernon could do nothing but stare. Numerous occasions in his line of work had seen him defuse situations before they escalated into all-out violence. He'd seen it all from the satin-shirted peacocking young men to strapping gym rats sporting thick muscle in tight T-shirts. Regardless of the type of nightclub patron, Vernon could read them all well enough – from the exaggerated swagger in their walk to a backward glance and grin at their posse (and thus avoiding excessive eye contact with the doormen). The boy in his flat exhibited none of the physicality or nuances expected from a normal human being. *Human?* Vernon's mind pondered the word in revulsion. The thing in his flat was anything but.

The trembling that there had been in his legs now graduated to a full-body tremor. Slivers of pain raced along his neck and arms, and the air in the room suddenly seemed thinner. Vernon dropped his gaze slightly to the boy's chest, looking for a sign of respiration – anything to convince him the nightmare was just in his mind.

The image on the TV vanished with a muffled *fmpff,* disappearing in a diffuse white star fading to black, and the overhead light gave a subdued pop before plunging the room into darkness. Whatever homeliness the flat had held fell away beneath the incessant patter of rain from outside the building, drumming on the roof and pattering outside the window. Vernon's eyes gradually adjusted, but with the room illuminated only by the weak evening light from outside, dappled by the rain, the boy remained in silhouette and shadow. He was sure the boy was closer to him now, although he hadn't seen or heard him move.

'Better?'

Vernon turned to run, tripped over his own feet and fell across the doorway with a heavy thud, knocking the wind out of himself. His phone slipped from his hand and tumbled out of reach. Pain continued to race along his neck and arms – his legs too now – and his hands and feet began to feel unnaturally numb and weak. His breathing hitched in his chest, each breath short, fast and shallow. He began to sob.

The door to his left opened with the lethargic pace of honey poured from a spoon: the very door he only used when he would impress his guests with his revered and sacred vinyl collection and precision turntablism.

No, no, no, no, no…

The boy exited the room *(but he was in the lounge!)* and walked toward him at the same unhurried pace. Vernon felt his bladder let go, feeling a brief flicker of relief as urine left him, soaking his shorts. Sodden fabric held to him like cling film.

Small and neat polished shoes stopped well within his field of vision. Vernon sensed rather than saw that the boy had hitched up his jeans like a suited city-worker before squatting beside him.

'You want to leave.' It wasn't a question.

Vernon had passed beyond alarm and fear; he was truly *petrified*. There was no escaping that sinister boy and that awful, feathery whisper. He clenched his jaw in a futile effort to drown out the voice. Hands scrabbling like spiders, he dug uselessly at the hallway carpet.

'There is nothing left for you. There is *no one* left but you.'

A desperate glance for an escape route in the twilight gloom revealed nothing useful except the blurred outline of his phone, far out of reach. Vernon struggled to turn away when pain flowered in his chest.

Darkness clouding his vision, the dust in the carpet drifting into his airway.

As did the smell of wet earth.

SUNDAY SUPPER

Vanessa Reid

"Where are you going?" Elijah's mother frowned as she watched him walk down the cabin's front steps with a walking stick in his hand. "There's still a lot to unpack."

Elijah looked back at his mother; she was trying to balance a box of mismatched dishes and an old broom. Everything old from their house in Cartersville was coming to the cabin for a second life. His daddy joked that it was his second life, too.

"I'm going exploring, Momma. Daddy said I should. He said I was a good helper and to go be a boy in the woods." He looked down at the ground and poked a dead leaf with his walking stick, waiting for his mother's reaction.

She sighed and softened. "Okay, baby. You have been a good helper. Go on, but take Athena with you, and don't get lost. Be home before dinner."

Elijah looked up at her and grinned. "You're a good one, Momma. Athena! Come on, girl." The chocolate lab nosed the screen door and trotted down the steps to his side, wagging her tail manically.

The boy and his dog took off into the woods, and his mother's smile faded to a frown as she watched after them until she couldn't see them any longer.

* * *

Elijah, an effortless tracker like his father, picked through the woods, following a faint trail toward the east. Athena trotted in front of him. Absently, Elijah began to sing. His mother always said he sang like an angel. His father said that boys don't sing except in church. Elijah asked him, "But what about Elvis?" His answer was a good-natured smack against his head.

"A mighty fortress is our God,
a bulwark never failing."

Athena nipped at a blue butterfly, leaping after nothing as the dainty insect spiraled out of the dog's reach. Athena barked at it for good measure. "Thena! Don't you bark at that little thing. She hasn't done anything to you."

"Our helper he, amid the flood,
of mortal ills prevailing."

The pair headed deeper into a stand of scrubby pine trees, and Elijah took in the things around him: scaly old trees, fallen skeletal branches, and shamelessly full ferns preening up through the packed earth. He inhaled deeply and smelled the moist, fresh rot and the sappy pine. He felt his body relax the farther he walked into the woods with his best friend leading the way.

"For still our ancient foe
does seek to work us woe;
his craft and power are great,
and armed with cruel hate,
on earth is not his equal—"

"Athena!" The dog stopped abruptly, almost causing the boy to trip over her. "What are you doing?" Athena did not look at Elijah. She took one step forward, broadening her stance, and started in on a low growl as she stared straight ahead.

Elijah looked up and around, surveying the area. He could see nothing, hear nothing, but Athena could. Elijah's heart pounded as he realized the trail they had followed from the cabin no longer existed.

"Thena?" he whispered. "What is it, girl?"

A twig snapped, and a tiny movement up ahead made Athena's hackles rise, and she began to bark and growl in a garbled warning.

"Who's there?" Elijah asked. The small, thin boy held his walking stick up in front of him. It was a sad weapon.

"Show yourself!" he braved.

The sun slid a fraction and blistered through the dense trees as a shape emerged through the glare. Elijah put his hand to his eyes and watched as a fae, feminine figure moved toward him hesitantly through the fleeting bright light. Then, at once, the sun sank another fraction and was blocked again by the trees. As the light died around her, Elijah could see that it was a human girl with messy blonde hair, a heart-shaped face, and small breasts. Elijah blushed. She was a pretty, human girl, but a girl, just the same. Well, maybe a girl-woman, he thought. He couldn't tell exactly how old she was. Elijah relaxed a little. Athena did not.

"Who are you?" Elijah asked, still brandishing his weapon.

The girl looked at Elijah and sized him up, taking in his small size. She, too, seemed to relax. "Why, you're just a little boy!" she said, her voice warm and unexpectedly raspy.

Elijah's anxiety flashed to anger. "I am NOT a *little boy*! I'm almost thirteen. Not some baby," he frowned.

The girl grinned and tilted her head to better look at Elijah. "No. You are not a baby. I'm sorry if I hurt your feelings. You just didn't *look* thirteen from a distance. But I can tell, now. Definitely." She smiled.

Elijah eyed her for a moment and decided that she had made up for the slight. He smiled cautiously. "I'm Elijah, and this is Athena." He gestured to the dog.

"Hi, Elijah . . . and Athena. My name is June. Are you all new to the mountain? I've never seen you before."

"My Daddy and Momma just bought the old green cabin back that way." He gestured west. "The only problem is, there aren't other people out here. I'm happy to meet someone else who lives here. All the neighbor cabins are empty."

June frowned. "That's probably because of what happened."

Elijah glanced at June and frowned. "What happened?" he repeated.

She looked at him gravely. "You don't know?"

Elijah shook his head.

"About nine years ago, some kids started going missing around here. First, there was a little girl who got lost in the woods. Her parents stopped down the highway at a rest stop, and she wandered off. They never found her," June said.

"Later, twins. A boy and a girl, I think about five years old. They were taken in the night from their campsite over in Morganton. Poof. Gone. Then, for the next six years or so, kids just disappeared. Vanished without a trace…seven in all. There were searches and dogs," June glanced at Athena, "but they never found them. People were scared and sold their cabins and moved away. Then, about two years ago, no more kids went missing. It just stopped. I guess people still don't want to come back here. That's my guess, anyway," she said as she glanced at something on the ground.

Elijah shivered. "That *is* a story. Geez. Those little kids. I bet they were so scared. Boy, I'm glad it's over, though. I wouldn't want to live here with a child kidnapper on the loose."

"You mean a child *killer*," June said darkly.

"Yeah, I guess so," Elijah fidgeted.

June smiled. "Hey. Wanna see something good?"

Elijah nodded.

"Good. Follow me."

June turned on her heel in dirty, old work boots that were several sizes too large, but she strolled off confidently, and Elijah followed her. For a moment, Athena hesitated, but when she realized her master was going without her, she followed closely behind.

* * *

June led Elijah and Athena first east, then south; she knew these woods like the back of her hand. They walked and talked easily for about half an hour until June stopped short of an outcropping of large rocks. "Shhh." June put her finger to her lips, gesturing for quiet. Then, she signaled Elijah to follow her as she scaled the pile of rocks. Athena remained on the ground, never taking her eyes off Elijah.

June tiptoed to a tree that split the rocky structure as they reached the top, and she peered into a tangle of twigs and pine straw. She pointed dramatically at the nest, grabbing Elijah's hand and pulling him to look.

Elijah glanced down, and he heard the soft squeaks before he saw the baby birds opening their tiny beaks in anticipation of their mother. They bobbed their bald heads and seemed to sing: *We're hungry! We're hungry!* Elijah stared. *Such little things and they are all alone.*

"Wow," he breathed quietly, never taking his eyes from the little piebald birds.

"Aren't they amazing?" June whispered, smiling at Elijah's pleasure. "We can't stay long, though. The momma will be back with dinner soon, and we'll scare her off."

Elijah nodded absently, still staring at the birds. Then June's words registered. *Dinner! How late was it?* He looked up at June and whispered, "I have to go, too. My momma will skin me alive if I'm late."

June nodded and gestured for Elijah to follow. They climbed down the rocks and away from the outcropping until they reached a safe distance to talk.

"That was something, June!"

"Aren't they amazing?"

"They sure are. How'd you ever find that nest up there?"

June glanced away. "Papa's a tracker and a hunter. He knows everything about the woods. He taught me how to find and cover tracks. He taught me how to find anything and to hunt it down if I need to."

Elijah nodded.

A crow cawed in the distance. "I can show you all

kinds of things." June watched Elijah. "Hey? Do you want to go fishing with me tomorrow? I know a great little spot on the river where you can catch more trout than you can eat. It's the prettiest place you've ever seen."

"That sounds great!" Elijah grinned as June reached down and scratched Athena between her ears in just the right spot. The dog finally gave in, squinting happily. June and Elijah giggled as Athena grunted her satisfaction.

* * *

June asked, "Do you have any brothers or sisters?" as they walked back to their meeting spot.

"Naw. I'm an only child. I've always wanted a sister, though. Do you have a sister or a brother?"

"Yes, two sisters! And four brothers, and there is a baby, too! We're a big family," she smiled.

"Wow, that *is* a big family. You're lucky," he frowned. "It gets lonely being the only one, you know?"

June nodded. "Yes, I know. But you've got me now. I'll be your sister," she smiled, and his heart soared.

"I'd like that."

They planned their fishing expedition for the next day. June led Elijah to where they met, and agreed to pick him up in the same spot first thing in the morning. She would bring the bait, and he would bring snacks.

"Where's your cabin?" Elijah asked.

June pointed west. "Over that way. Just past that ridge, and then you've got to cross Baker's creek, but it's hard to find. Papa likes his privacy. Let's just meet here like we planned, okay?"

Elijah nodded and said he could find his way home

from there. He said goodbye and tripped lightly back to the cabin with Athena at his side. June watched him and hugged herself as she felt the coolness of evening set in. Then, she headed back into the woods.

∗ ∗ ∗

Elijah wasn't late for supper, and he sat at the rickety cabin table, munching happily on his hamburger. His mother said they would eat picnic food until Sunday supper, and he was just fine with that. He shoved three french fries into his mouth. The crinkle cut. His favorite.

"Well, Elijah, how was your walk in the woods? See anything good?" his father asked.

"Yeah, I did. I met a friend. She was nice. She showed me a baby birds' nest and everything! We're gonna go fishing tomorrow."

"Well, I'm glad you met another child," his mother said. "It could be lonely out here for you when your daddy is hunting with his buddies and no one to keep you company but your old mother." His mother smiled and winked at him.

"I guess," said his father. "Is she pretty?"

Elijah blushed.

"Oh, she is, isn't she!" his father whooped.

"Yes, sir," Elijah smiled now. His parents had accepted the idea of June and didn't tell him that he couldn't go fishing tomorrow.

"She also told me about the bad thing that happened."

His mother looked up. "The bad thing?"

His father shifted in his chair.

"About the missing kids. June told me that a bunch of

kids went missing a few years ago but that it stopped, and everything was okay now. It's all over." Elijah shoved another fist full of fries into his mouth.

Elijah's mother frowned. "Did you know about this, Douglas?" Elijah noted that his mother only called his father "Douglas" when she was mad.

"Now, Janie, don't go getting riled up. Yes. I had heard about the troubles near here, but that was years ago, and like Elijah said, it's all over. The realtor said whoever took those kids was dead or long gone. There's nothing to worry about."

"You should have told me."

"I didn't think it was a big deal. It doesn't affect us, and we got a good deal. I knew it would worry you, but there's nothing to worry about."

"That's a lot of reasons not to tell me, Douglas."

Elijah's father sighed. "I'm sorry, Janie. I *should* have told you."

His mother made a slight nod of acceptance and then stood to clear the table in silence. She would be like that until at least tomorrow, Elijah thought. But even the tension between his parents couldn't dampen his spirits. He was going fishing with June tomorrow, after all.

* * *

The following day, Elijah tripped lightly down the cabin steps as he headed out to meet June. He couldn't help smiling and humming as he walked through the forest, Athena at his side.

The cheerful sun disappeared behind a cloud for a moment, and the woods grew dim and still. A murder of crows argued in the near distance, and a branch snapped and fell to the forest floor.

Elijah stopped and looked around. "June?" The crows went silent. "Are you there?"

The sun broke out from behind the cloud and lit his path. At the same moment, Athena spotted a squirrel and trotted happily after it. The spell was broken, and Elijah relaxed a bit and continued.

Elijah found June at their spot, and he showed her his fishing pole and the contents of his satchel. His mother had made them egg salad sandwiches on homemade rye bread and a thermos of chocolate milk. June nodded approvingly, and they were off.

June led Elijah to the spot on the river, and as promised, it was the prettiest place he had ever seen. The water curved inward on a perfect shallow where they could stand and cast comfortably, protected from the sun by a shelter of river birches. Verbena bushes dotted the shore, showing off their purple fruit, and butterflies danced in the leaves of a large bottle brush bush. Elijah said he thought it looked like a vacation postcard, and June giggled in agreement.

As they prepared their poles with June's bait, Elijah began to sing softly to himself.

"And though this world, with devils filled,
should threaten to undo us,
we will not fear, for God has willed
his truth to triumph through us.
The prince of darkness grim,
we tremble not for him;
his rage we can endure,

for lo! his doom is sure;
one little word shall fell him.”

He looked up. June was staring at him. “That was beautiful,” she breathed.

Elijah blushed. He hadn’t realized that he was singing. “It’s a church song, ‘A Mighty Fortress is Our God.’ I sing in the boys’ choir,” he added sheepishly.

“You have the loveliest voice I’ve ever heard.” Her smile faded. “Do you think that’s true?”

Elijah beamed. “What’s true?”

“Do you think *one little word* will stop the Prince of Darkness?”

“Oh, shoot yeah! God can do anything. Just like the song says:

“God’s truth abideth still;
his kingdom is forever!” he sang.

June looked down at her fishing pole. “I wish I could be as sure as you. Your voice almost makes me believe it.” She smiled sadly at him. “I don’t think anything can stop the Prince of Darkness. Even God.”

Elijah looked at her but could think of nothing to say. He sensed the depth of her sadness, and it was a sick, dark thing. Too deep for a pretty girl like June. Instinctively, he put down his fishing pole and put his arms around her, holding her close. She was warm and soft against him, and his face reddened as he felt her breasts through her flannel shirt. She stood rigid for a moment but then began to tremble. She grabbed hold of Elijah, and she sobbed softly.

Elijah had never held a girl before and certainly not a

crying one. He let her go on and felt so much grief pour out of her that it scared him, but he didn't dare ask where it came from. He just held her until her sobs ebbed to a sigh and she pulled away.

"Thank you. I'm sorry."

Elijah shook his head. "Don't be sorry. There's nothing to be sorry about. I wish I could take away that sadness you've got inside of you."

June smiled at Elijah and wiped her eyes. "I wish you could, too. Come on. Let's get some fish for dinner. I bet you'll make your daddy proud if you bring home a whopper!"

Elijah grinned and nodded, and they fished in companionable silence, only pausing to eat lunch. June gobbled up four of the six egg salad sandwiches, declaring Elijah's mother's egg salad the best she'd ever had. Elijah grinned. He'd never seen a girl eat like that, but he'd never met a girl quite like June.

* * *

Elijah brought home four fat trout, and his father smiled and clapped him on the back the way he did his hunting buddies. Elijah glowed. His mother fussed over having to clean the fish but was pleased dinner would be something other than hotdogs or hamburgers. "You better bring that little girl home next time so that we can meet her," his mother said. "I can send her home with some cornbread." He smiled and said he would.

"How about you and me go take a look at that acreage next door tomorrow? I heard it's for sale," his father said. "We can check out the property line and see if we like it."

Elijah grinned.

Elijah's mother rolled her eyes but smiled good-naturedly. She was finished being angry with her husband after late-night reassurances that the cabin and the woods were safe.

Glancing out the window, she said, "You better hope those storm clouds move on, or the only thing you'll be doing tomorrow is painting that back room while I get Sunday supper ready. Say, why don't you invite your friend to join us for supper tomorrow?"

"Really? Are you sure, Momma?" Elijah beamed. "That'd be great!"

Elijah's momma smiled.

"Janie, is that contentment I see on your pretty face? I thought you hated this old cabin?" Elijah's father smirked.

"Oh, I suppose so. Elijah sure likes it, and the peace and quiet is kinda growing on me, I guess."

Elijah and his father smiled at one another, both delighted in her change of heart.

* * *

It rained all Sunday morning. Elijah paced the cabin, driving his mother crazy as she unpacked the fresh vegetables and ham she'd managed to find at a farmers' market in town. "Go on and help your father. You two need to get at least that backroom started. It's not going to paint itself."

"Oh, alright."

Elijah helped his father tape up and prime the small room in the back of the cabin, frequently glancing out the window at the rain coming down.

Just after lunch, the rain stopped. The sky remained threatening, but it was no longer too wet to go out and find June. Elijah brightened, announced his plan, and promised to be home in time for Sunday supper. He flew down the cabin stairs with Athena in tow.

* * *

"June?" Elijah stood in their meeting spot, listening to the raindrops fall from the trees onto springy ferns that seemed to puff and grow in the moisture. A rotting smell was compounded by the fetid dampness that made Elijah dizzy. He waited, feeling the drips on his head, and he began to shiver from the dropping temperature that followed the early summer storm. Athena paced at Elijah's feet, adding to his discomfort and growing impatience.

"Settle down, girl," he snapped. Athena sighed and plopped down at his feet. Elijah didn't know why he assumed June would just appear. She had before, but she wasn't expecting him. Well, Elijah would just have to find her. He knew the general direction of her cabin. Besides, he had plenty of time before supper, so he set off toward the ridge and headed west.

* * *

Elijah stopped to get his bearings. This section of the woods was different. The trees were denser, and strange sounds popped and fluttered. Things he couldn't see. "June?" Athena, too, was on high alert, and Elijah's heart beat loudly. Elijah pushed on when there was no reply, moving more quickly and looking over his shoulder often.

Twenty minutes later, Elijah felt he must be close. His father often said his son's sense of direction was better than a homing pigeon on a clear day. *Baker's Creek!* He trotted across the rocks, clearing the creek in seconds. He continued as the brush became denser and more difficult to navigate. Following the sun had become increasingly difficult, too, as the trees were taller, reaching spiny limbs to the sky, reaching for something.

After he passed through a particularly dense group of trees, the forest opened up into a large, ragged clearing. At first, he couldn't see anything unusual. Then, a sharp corner. He could see the edge of a small building up ahead, and he and Athena jogged along merrily to find its door.

The wooden structure was smaller than a house but more substantial than a shed. He knew that it couldn't be June's house; it even looked abandoned, but curiosity got the better of him, and he walked up the sagging stairs. At first, the rusty doorknob wouldn't give, but Elijah gave the door a hearty shove with his hip, and the door swung open.

Elijah and Athena stepped inside and were assaulted by a choking, dusty stillness and an appalling smell. He pulled his T-shirt up over his face and surveyed the small room noting a work table, an old circular saw, and a large variety of tools hanging from a pegboard wall above the dusty table. It was oddly bright despite the dirty windows, but the piles of junk and old boxes covered in gray dust showed the workshop had not been used in some time. *Who would come in here?* Elijah thought. *That smell!* That's when he noticed a large pile of fur near the workbench. He peered a little closer and could see it was a rat that appeared to have died recently. Its body had just begun to cave in, and flies still circled its corpse. Elijah wondered if it had gotten in and couldn't get out. *Poor thing.*

Elijah frowned and turned to leave but paused when something else caught his eye. Behind a mound of junk, he could see a swatch of red peeking between a stack of Georgia peaches boxes and a pile of faded blankets. He walked around the tipsy heap and found the source of the strangely vibrant color. Elijah gasped, and Athena leaped to investigate.

A man lay on the floor wearing a red flannel shirt and dirty blue jeans, but he wasn't a man anymore. What lay before Elijah was a dead man whose drying bones sagged loosely against the floor, with bits of black, dried muscle and skin still clinging in gruesome leathery patches. He was lying on his stomach with his head turned to the side, and his mouth was hanging open. Also, there was an ax embedded deeply in the back of his skull. Withering, dirty brown hair framed the blade and clung to the corpse's skull. Athena circled the body, pacing and sniffing frantically, her tail wagging low in cautious alarm.

Elijah's stomach lurched, and he turned and ran out of the workshop and out into the sunlight. He hunched over, breathing heavily, trying to expel the putrid smell from his nose and mouth. Athena ran out after him and licked his arm as he squatted down on his knees. "It's okay, girl. It's okay," he reassured her, but it wasn't. Elijah's mind reeled as his body trembled.

Then, he heard something. A tittering carried on the breeze. At first, he thought it was a bird calling, but the voice became decidedly human. Laughter. A girl's laughter. June's laughter. He stood and looked around frantically for its source, wanting to tell June, to warn her about the thing inside the workshop. He spotted a rusty slip of metal through the trees. *A roof. It must be June's house*, he thought. He had to warn her.

Elijah ran toward the old cabin, which had been well-hidden by a line of scrub pines, but once he was upon it, he hesitated as he could hear June chatting happily through the open front windows. He walked to the door.

"And why should you get an extra helping of mashed potatoes, Billy? You were very naughty this morning when I asked you to get dressed, and you ran out into the woods to play in your pajamas! I should have spanked you right there. More potatoes? I don't think so," she chastised gently.

"Thomas! Do not touch your sister's plate. You were not raised in a barn!"

Elijah smiled. His mother said that all of the time. He must have stumbled upon Sunday supper at June's house. The normalcy of this moment blurred his memory of the dead man in the workshop for a moment.

Elijah ran his fingers through his hair and brushed off his shirt. He didn't want to look like a mess when he met June's family. He walked up the cabin's steps, and that's when he noticed that there was a screen door, and the front door was wide open, letting in the stingy summer breeze. The screen was rusty, and the room inside was dark, so he couldn't see much until he got up to it and peered into June's cabin. Then, his smile faded.

Elijah opened the screen door silently and stepped into the cabin with Athena quiet at his feet. If the sight of the dead man had confounded him before, his brain worked feverishly to understand this.

June, wearing a gingham apron, walked around a large round dining table with an empty pot in her hand as she spooned air onto plates dotted with twigs and leaves. "No, no, Jamie," she said. "You don't start eating until I sit down and we say the blessing, remember?" June turned to the small kitchen behind her and put down the pot on the cold stove. Then, she took off her apron and placed it on a hook by the window.

Elijah made a slight sound in his throat as he looked around the table, and June turned to see him standing in front of her door. "Elijah!"

Elijah stared at the table in disbelief. It was set for seven with what he assumed was June's empty chair. Strange, silent guests occupied the other six seats. Children. There were six skeleton children sitting around the table strapped to their chairs with duct tape that appeared to hold up their haggard remains.

For a moment, Elijah thought they were Halloween decorations like the ones his friend Robert put around his house in October. Then he remembered the man in the workshop. They looked like him, but they were all bones.

Elijah's mind worked to understand. Next to June's seat, there appeared to be two children dressed identically in blue tops with red whales on them. What little hair was left looked like dusty blonde curls.

A year later, twins. A boy and a girl, I guess about five years old.

Around the rest of the table sat four more similarly withered children of various ages in faded and tattered clothing.

There were seven in all.

Six dead children. And June.

Elijah looked up at June. She stood watching him as tears rolled down her cheeks, and he felt her bottomless agony like a punch in the stomach. June stood before him in her oversized men's shirt and too-large work boots. She looked so fragile, so beautiful, standing there in the weak sunlight coming through the kitchen window. Not like the girl in the woods. Not like his friend June.

First, it was a little girl who got lost in the woods.

Elijah's tears started as he looked around again at her "family" and their Sunday supper. He remembered the dead man in the workshop. He remembered the ax in his head. The owner of June's shirt and work boots. The man who used to live in this house.

Then, about two years ago, no more kids went missing. It just stopped.

Elijah went to June and put his arms around her. Athena trotted over and stood at her feet. June stood rigid for a moment but then gave in and sobbed from her bones. Elijah held her tight, knowing that if he didn't, she would go away forever.

Without thinking, Elijah began to hum a familiar tune to comfort June, and he thought about the last verse:

"Let goods and kindred go,
this mortal life also;
the body they may kill:
God's truth abideth still;
his kingdom is forever!"*

As Elijah held June, he looked around again at the macabre scene before him. All of these poor children.

---

* *"A Mighty Fortress Is Our God" by Martin Luther (1529)*

And June, hosting an endless, make-believe supper to keep them, and herself, from disappearing forever.

Then, to the right of June's chair, Elijah saw the hardest sight yet. A wooden vegetable box perched on an old stool with peeling red paint. A tiny human skeleton, the size of a newborn infant, was in the box, wrapped in a faded yellow blanket. Elijah's heart sank even further. There was an eighth child, but it was June's.

June's sobs quieted, but she slumped in his arms. He pulled back gently, still holding her, and he looked questioningly into her haunted eyes.

"Papa," she gestured toward the workshop, "Papa took me when I was little. Said he wanted a daughter and that God sent me. He made me call him 'Papa,' even though I knew I had a daddy and a momma somewhere else. He said he wanted more children. He told me how to talk to them and bring them to him. Then, he took them. He hurt them," she sobbed and paused for a moment.

"One day, he said he didn't need a daughter anymore. He said he needed a wife, and he put a baby inside me. When he hurt that baby…I couldn't let him do it anymore. I just couldn't!" Elijah nodded and held on to June, who gazed into the past.

"Then, one day, when he went into the shed, I followed him. He kept his tools there, but one was missing. I hid that ax under the front step, and I followed him. Didn't you sing, 'One little word shall fell him'?

"I snuck up behind him, and I took that ax, and I brought it down on him. I felled him. He never even looked back. He always told me I was the quietest tracker he'd ever met. Then it was over." She looked at Elijah, her body shaking. "It is over, isn't it?"

He nodded. "Yes, June. It's all over now. You're going to come home with me, you hear? It's going to be alright. Momma's got Sunday supper ready. Okay? You're coming with me. Do you understand?"

June blinked at Elijah and looked at her family around the table. "What about them? I can't just leave them. They need me."

"Don't worry, June, we'll come back for them, okay?"

June turned to Elijah, her eyes focused, and she nodded. Elijah took her hand, and he and Athena led her home.

THE TRUE AND SHORT LIFE OF A WEREWOLF

Augustus Stephens

J oe lifted his umbrella and poked the dog in its eye. The beast yelped, and in so doing let go of Joe's leg. It turned around and loped off into the darkness.

Joe staggered a little and sat on a nearby wall. He looked down at his leg, a little blood was visible and it bloody hurt, but it seemed alright. He found that he could walk it off.

When he got home he took off his trousers and inspected the wound. There were deep tooth marks, but no other damage. Joe felt sure his up-to-date tetanus shots would do and he didn't consider going to the doctor.

* * *

Three and a half weeks later he stood in his kitchen in the evening with a cup of decaf coffee in his hand and thought back to the incident. Who would let such a dangerous animal loose on the streets? Perhaps he should have notified the police. He noticed the moon coming out from behind some clouds, it looked full, and then he started to feel strangely hot.

A sudden pain gripped him in the belly; he thought that he might be going to be sick. It felt like his insides were churning. He doubled up with the pain. He was sweating like a pig. He undid the buttons on his shirt and ripped it off. He didn't know why he did that. A soft moan escaped from his lips.

Now he was on the floor on all fours, gasping for breath. He crawled across the kitchen to the downstairs loo, but when he got there he just lay on the floor. He screamed with the pain that was now in his head and legs and chest and everywhere. He undid his jeans and pushed them off him; then he just ripped his underpants off. That felt a little better.

The pain which had been bad suddenly ramped up another notch and left tears running from his eyes. He couldn't even scream anymore; it was too much. Then he blacked out.

On opening his eyes he was on all fours in the toilet, panting. He looked around and found that his hands were now paws and his body was furry and there was a long nose poking out of his face in front of his eyes; in fact he was a big dog, or possibly a wolf.

Strangely he didn't find this odd. It just felt like he had found his true self.

He padded out into the kitchen, put his paw on the door handle, pulled down and opened the door. He crept out into the night. It felt good; it felt right. He looked at the moon and gave a mournful hoooowwwwl. Then he jumped over the fence at the bottom of the garden, went along the lane and into the street. There was no one about.

He padded down the streets, round a few corners. Somehow he felt like he knew where he was going. Then he turned another corner and saw what it was that was drawing him. A wood.

* * *

Ginger was a rabbit. A white rabbit. She had no say over her name. That was due to Bernadette who, when she learned she was to get a rabbit, was determined to call it Ginger, come what may.

It was an evening like any other, and Ginger had finished eating her green pellets and was wondering what to do with herself that long night. It was the nights that were worst, for when she felt most awake and hungered to be sniffling around the vegetables in the garden she was always locked inside her hutch.

On this evening she pushed at the door of the hutch, knowing that it would be locked as always, when she found that it gave. The door moved. She pushed it some more with her nose and it swung outwards smoothly. The door was open. Escape was possible.

She hopped down and sniffed and looked around. No one was about.

She went over to the vegetable patch and nibbled at a carrot top. How she loved carrot tops! It was delicious.

She wondered about the other vegetables, but there was a raw and exciting smell coming to her nostrils; she went to the bottom of the garden, crawled under the hedge and poked her nose out. There she saw the most amazing and beautiful thing – a wood. So many scents assailed her nose. So much room beckoned to her, her true home. She hopped into the wood and nibbled on a leaf.

So fresh, so raw, so tasty. She had to have more of this. She went on exploring.

In time she came to a glade with soft, lush grass and a big oak tree at its centre. What a delightful scene! What a place to find! And there, in the grass, nibbling away, was a clutch of rabbits.

Ginger was nervous. These were real, wild rabbits and she hadn't met another rabbit since the time she was a tiny kit.

One of the wild, brown rabbits saw her and cautiously hopped over. They looked at each other face to face for a few moments. Ginger felt a strange stirring in her loins. There was something about this rabbit she found intoxicating. The two rabbits circled each other briefly and then they met like an explosion.

Ginger had never had sex before, never even dreamt of such a thing, but it felt the most delirious and wonderful magic she had ever known. In a few moments it was over and she hopped into the pack of rabbits, a fully fledged member of the warren. She nibbled on the wondrous fresh grass along with the others.

* * *

Joe the Wolf sniffed and could sense the scent of wildlife, in particular of rabbits. He put his nose to the floor and followed the scent through the trees. He came to an elderly oak standing in a glade, with gnarled roots and between the roots a selection of holes. The scent from the holes told him there were rabbits down there. Real, live rabbits. But they were far underground beneath the roots. The rabbits would know he was there too. He crawled under a nearby bush, put his head on his paws and set to wait.

After what seemed an age his keen eyes saw a nose poke out from one of the holes. Then after the nose came a head and at last a rabbit hopped out. The animal stood by the oak tree and sniffed and looked round and round. It hopped a couple of times then started to nibble at the grass growing in the glade. More rabbits came hopping out, all rather nervous, but each would eventually start nibbling at the grass.

The rabbits spread out.

Strangely, one of the rabbits to come out of the burrow wasn't the usual brown but a snowy white. This rabbit seemed less cautious and it ventured closer to where Joe the Wolf was hiding.

The white rabbit nibbled at some bramble leaves. It picked carefully at the young and tender leaves avoiding the prickles. Occasionally stopping, looking up and around and sniffing the air.

Joe the Wolf lay still, tense with excitement, in his hiding spot downwind of the burrow.

As the white rabbit made another couple of hops towards Joe, he was suddenly all movement. His powerful hind legs made him surge forward at an astonishing rate; the rabbit literally jumped in the air with surprise, turning as it did so. Joe heard its little paws thump the ground as it landed, ready to run back to the safety of the burrow, but the little creature was too close to the ravenous wolf. Joe was on it in a fraction of a second. His jaws closed over its back and he bit down hard. He heard the spine crunch and the rabbit went limp in his jaws.

Joe the Wolf put the rabbit carcass down and tried to eat it by tearing the flesh from its side, but the thing was so light he just picked it up again. He held the rabbit down with a paw and ripped the flesh from its flank. He did the same for the legs, feeling the warm flesh and blood as it went over his tongue and down his gullet. Then he tore the carcass apart and chomped and chewed and ground and gnawed each piece until he could swallow it down.

Now he felt better. He licked his lips with his long tongue. He didn't feel so desperate for food, but a rabbit is so small. He was still hungry.

He settled himself under the bush again to wait for the other rabbits to come out again.

Having not slept since the previous night, Joe the Wolf's eyes slowly closed. He jerked them open, but no sign of rabbits. His eyelids closed again and Joe the Wolf drifted off into a contented sleep.

* * *

When he woke he felt very cold. He was shivering. He opened his eyes to find that it was now light and that his paws were hands, his legs were arms and he didn't have a great nose constantly in his vision. In fact, he was a cold, naked man lying under a bush in the woods.

He crawled out from the bush and stood up. Boy, was he cold! He jumped up and down a bit to warm up. Then he picked his way carefully among the leaves and brambles and headed for the road.

When he got to the edge of the wood the sun was just coming up over the rooftops; it was very early morning.

He had to get home.

He had to get home unseen.

He went through the kissing gate and stood on the pavement opposite a line of houses. He looked left and he looked right and he looked at the houses. No one on the street, no curtains open in the houses. Everyone was asleep.

He started walking back towards home. He turned right into a street lined both sides with houses, keeping his eyes and ears open. The surface of this pavement was rough with stones sticking through the tarmac and his walking slowed as he tried to cope with the pain of each footfall.

He heard a car behind him, he looked back to see one turning into his street, and he quickly ran through a gateway and crouched down behind the hedge. The car drove down the road and passed him then turned again at the other end of the road.

He continued his walk homewards.

At the end of the road he turned left round a high privet hedge and came face to face with a lady walking a dog. He stopped and said 'Good morning' brightly. The lady said 'Good morning' back and the border collie sniffed at Joe's privates. 'He's always doing that,' apologised the lady and Joe stepped around the dog and carried on. He noticed a few houses had their curtains drawn, but what could he do?

Just as he reached the turning at the end of that road a car came round the corner. It was a police car. Joe stood still. Two policewomen got out of the car

'Out for a stroll are we, sir?' asked one of them.

'Yes,' said Joe.

'So what happened to your clothes?'

'I - I - I was sleepwalking,' said Joe.

The policewoman looked sceptical.

'No really,' said Joe. 'I just woke up.'

'Hmmm,' said the policewoman. 'Can I have your name and address?'

Joe told her.

She got on her radio and asked for them to look up the name. The reply came that there was no record of him.

'Well, are you planning on going far?'

'No,' said Joe. 'I'm just going home.'

'Well,' said the policewoman, 'perhaps it would be better if we gave you a lift. Would that be agreeable?'

'Oh, indeed,' said Joe.

She opened the back door of the car. 'If you'd just like to step inside.'

'No,' said the other policewoman. 'I'm not having him sit on the seat like that. That car's practically new. I'm not having his hairy arse on my new seats.'

'My arse isn't hairy,' said Joe.

'And you can shut it, chap, or you'll be arrested instead of given a lift home,' responded the surly policewoman.

The first policewoman looked vexed. She went to the back of the car and opened the boot. She rummaged around and pulled out a blanket. 'Ah, this is just the thing.' She handed it to Joe. 'If you don't mind?'

'Oh thank you,' he said and wrapped the blanket around himself then climbed into the back of the police car.

The policewomen got in the front and then drove round the next three corners until they were outside Joe's house. One of them got out and opened the rear door for him. He graciously handed the policewoman the blanket and strolled, whistling, into his garden and down the side alley to the back door, which was still open.

He went and put on a dressing gown then settled down with a cup of tea.

He began to shake, uncontrollably shake, and then he burst into tears.

* * *

Dylan liked weed. He lived for it. He didn't live by it; that would be silly and the road to destruction; at least, that's what he thought. He made a living doing the IT for a charity for adults with learning difficulties. It made him happy to be working for the good of people less fortunate than himself. But what made him happier still was weed.

Each evening he'd dip into his stash and go for a walk. He didn't dare smoke the stuff at home as his landlord had made it abundantly clear that drugs would not be tolerated, but Dylan didn't mind. It was nice to get out into the fresh air in the evening. It was good for the soul.

On this evening the air was still and warm and he headed to his favourite spot. A particular oak tree in a glade in a wood. It was like communing with nature as well as getting high. Ideal for the hippy that Dylan considered himself to be.

As he approached the oak he gave it a greeting, 'Hi there, Major Tom,' for that's what he called it. 'It's me, Dylan, come to see you again. Peace and love to you, dude.'

Then he sat down amongst the roots and carefully, religiously rolled an enormous spliff.

He lit it and sucked in deep. 'Why was this stuff illegal?' he mused to himself; the perfect drug and no one ever got angry or aggressive using it. It makes you feel relaxed and it makes you feel happy. He chuckled a bit and said, 'Major Tom, my mighty friend, this is some good shit I've got here. Good shit indeed.' He settled down and continued with his favourite pastime.

* * *

That night Joe stood in his kitchen and watched the moon rise over the rooftops opposite. He was wearing only a towel wrapped around his middle and he was shaking like a jelly.

At a moment that he couldn't predict, but which he had dreaded, he felt his stomach tighten and his chest squeeze and all the pain from the night before was repeated. He sprawled on the ground unable to bear it, but he had to bear it as his limbs shrunk and twisted, his face distorted and stretched, and fur grew from his body.

He stood panting in his kitchen, a fully formed wolf – and he was hungry.

He went out into the night to search for food. He wanted good, fresh meat.

He worked his way along the streets and found nobody there, just the occasional car driving past. What is it with this part of the town where nobody goes for a walk?

He came once more to the wood, hopped over the gate and made his way towards the oak tree with the rabbit warren.

When he got there he found there were no rabbits at

all; instead a man was sitting under the tree. Joe the Wolf detected the strong, pungent smell of cannabis.

'Yo, little doggie. Hello,' said the man under the tree.

Joe went up to him and looked at him.

The man tickled Joe the Wolf behind his right ear. 'You're a nice doggie, aren't you? What's your name?'

And Joe the Wolf opened his jaws and bit off the man's hand.

Dylan let out a grotesque scream that echoed all the way to the treetops, but there was no one to hear it.

Joe dropped the hand by the supine man and then ripped out his throat. Blood spurted up the trunk of the tree and once again Joe felt the delicious warmth of the flesh and blood as it coursed down his throat. He ripped the clothes off the man and dug in to the choicest bits. The thick muscles on his legs, the juicy buttocks and the fatty stomach. He gobbled and guzzled until he had had his fill; then he licked his lips and wiped his face with his paws until he was clean.

He sat down by the now destroyed carcass and went to sleep.

As he slept, some rabbits slipped out the back of their warren behind the oak tree and nibbled furtively on the grass.

* * *

Joe woke again as the sun was rising. Naked again. A man again. And he looked at the mess, the blood and bones scattered around, and he vomited.

But Joe had the same problem as last night. Once again, naked as the day he was born and in the woods.

But this time he felt differently. This time he didn't

care. He walked out onto the street boldly, not caring who saw him. As he turned the corner by the big hedge he found a police car parked on the street in front of him. For some reason he felt relieved.

The same two policewomen got out of the car as he approached it.

'Hello again,' said the surly one, 'thought we'd wait for you here just in case you needed us.'

'I d-do need you,' stammered Joe. 'I need help. I need to be locked up.'

'Well, that's lucky because you are going to be. I am arresting you for indecent exposure. You do not have to say anything, but it may harm your defence if you do not mention, when questioned, something you later rely on in court. Anything you do say may be given in evidence.' And she ushered him toward the back seat of the car, which already had a blanket lying on it. He got in.

When they got to the police station and he was in the reception to be processed they offered him a pair of tracksuit bottoms and a sweatshirt, which he gratefully accepted and put on.

'Do you know why you're here?' asked the desk sergeant.

'Yes,' said Joe, 'but there's more. I have to report that I committed murder last night.'

'Murder?' asked the desk sergeant.

'Yes. Cold blooded murder,' said Joe.

'Then I suppose I had better arrest you again,' said the surly policewoman. And she did so, using the new offence and repeating the famous words.'

'You can find the body in Baker's Wood,' said Joe; then he minutely described the location of the oak tree.

'Well, while we look into that we shall look after you here. Do you have any mental illness?'

'No,' said Joe. And the booking-in process continued until Joe was led down the corridor and put into cell A4C.

* * *

The time was precisely 08:02 and Detective Constable Rather marched into the office in a hurry. Two minutes late again, having spent the morning trying to console his daughter over the sudden loss of her rabbit.

He headed for his desk, but the sergeant called to him over the desk divider, 'Don't bother taking your coat off, Angus. We need you to go and look at something in the woods.'

'Oh?' said DC Rather.

'Yeah,' continued the sergeant. 'A man who was brought in claims he's murdered someone out in Baker's Wood. I don't think it's anything probably. They think he's not right in the head. Been wandering around last two nights as naked as a jay bird, but we have to check, don't we?'

'I should say so,' said DC Rather.

The sergeant gave him a slip of paper with the location described upon it and DC Rather headed off towards the car park.

* * *

DC Rather parked by the kissing gate and followed the instructions on his slip of paper: Along the path about two hundred yards then turn right by the fallen tree and continue on that path.

When he came to the glade with the oak tree his heart skipped a beat. He quickly got out his mobile and called the sergeant. 'Um. He's not a nut job, sarge. We've got an incident here. We're going to need a forensics team and all the works. It's carnage here.'

So the wheels of the Major Crimes Unit went into action and police cars, forensics crews and senior police officers turned up in their droves. Police tape was hung from tree to tree and little white tents went up in the glade as white-overalled operatives went about their grisly work.

* * *

By 17:52 Joe was sitting on one side of the table in Interview Room 2 in the custody suite at the police station, accompanied by the duty solicitor. On the other side were Detective Constable Rather and PC Martin.

'I just thought we'd have this quick meeting so you know where you stand, Mr Smith,' said DC Rather. 'The forensic team have been over the scene in the woods and they have concluded that you could have had nothing to do with it. It was clearly the work of a dog, a rabid dog or something. You are exonerated on that account.'

'But it was me,' said Joe. 'I was a wolf.'

'Yes,' said DC Rather, kindly.

'And as to the nudity charge, we're dropping that as well. We think you might be unwell, Mr Smith, and we've got an ambulance waiting outside to take you to the hospital where you can be looked after properly. It's not appropriate for you to be held in police cells if you're unwell.'

'But I'm dangerous and I need to be locked up,' said Joe.

'Well, we'll let the doctors decide on that, shall we? Do you want to follow PC Martin out now and the ambulance staff will take care of you?'

Still protesting, Joe followed PC Martin out of the custody suite and into the ambulance. Joe sat down on a chair accompanied by a paramedic and PC Martin got into a police car behind and followed the ambulance.

* * *

At the hospital he was taken into the Place of Safety where he was weighed, measured and inspected then left in a room with a sofa and a blanket, and he sat there alone while two nurses did who-knows-what in the office.

Joe stood at the window and looked at the garden outside as the sun went down, until later all he could see was a reflection of himself in the glass. Then he spied the moon rising above the rooftop opposite. He felt a gnawing in his belly and tears rolled down his cheeks.

He took off his clothes and waited. It happened just the same.

When he was a wolf he looked through the window again at the full moon and he howled. This caused one of the nurses to come out of the office and look into the room. They say curiosity killed the cat; well it isn't just cats. Joe the Wolf looked at the nurse, who was frozen on the spot, and then pounced.

He grabbed her leg in his powerful jaws and yanked her off her feet. He ripped a great slab of flesh from her thigh as the woman screamed and screamed. The other nurse put her head out of the staff room door then shut it as quick as lightning. Meanwhile, Joe the Wolf tore the flesh from the belly of the nurse who was on the floor. The screaming stopped as the woman lost consciousness. Joe hardly chewed the meat before swallowing it, and worked his way up the torso, taking the delicacy of the soft breasts and the smaller cuts on the arms in his stride. She was a delicious woman.

When he was sated he walked along the corridor, growling softly. He went to the entrance door and pushed. It didn't move. He tried the handle with his paw, but still nothing. He was locked in, so he turned his attention to the staff room.

* * *

Inside the staff room, Margaret Keeping was on the phone to the emergency police number. 'Help, help. You've got to help me. There's a gigantic dog in here and it's killed Precious.'

'Can you calm down, please? Tell me where you are and what's happened.'

Margaret took two deep breaths and started again, trying to keep the panic from her voice.

'Help is on its way,' said the call handler. 'I'll stay with you until it has arrived.'

'Oh thank you, thank you, thank you,' gasped Margaret.

Then there was an almighty thud on the staff room door.

'Oh god, it's trying to get in,' screamed Margaret down the phone.

* * *

Forty-nine minutes later, outside the Place of Safety was swarming with police and ambulances. Inspector Mark Cameron was in charge. He used his phone to get in contact with Margaret, who was still in the staff room inside.

'Margaret, Inspector Cameron here. Can you tell me the situation as it is now?'

'I'm still in the staff room, The dog or wolf or whatever it is has stopped banging the door and I think it's attacking the entrance door now.'

'Is that door locked?' asked the inspector.

'Yes, it is.'

'Can you unlock it from where you are?'

'No,' said Margaret. I have the key here with me, but the animal is out there.'

'Okay. Don't worry. We won't expect you to put yourself in any danger. Thank you, Margaret.'

He ended the call and walked up to the door in question. There was a great thud as something hurled itself at the door from the other side.

'It looks sturdy enough,' he said, 'but we should be able to break it down. Bring a ram.'

Police officers in bulletproof vests and protective helmets and gloves came up with the ram. Behind them gathered a small group of five firearms officers looking proud and confident.

The inspector arranged his troops.

'When the door opens, I want the ram team to run off to the left. I want the AFO team to wait six paces behind them with weapons ready. And everyone else I want out of the way. Back to your cars, ladies and gentlemen. I don't want any more casualties if this goes wrong.'

Everyone did as they were told.

The two men with the ram approached the door.

'On three,' said PC Starmer. 'One, two, three.' And they swung the ram forward. It cracked into the door, but the door held.

'Again. One, two, three.' The ram swung forward again and there was the sound of splitting wood and ripping metal, but the door seemed to hold.

Suddenly the door erupted outwards, pushing the two PCs with the ram to the floor and there stood Joe the Wolf. He stood and surveyed the scene, snarling angrily.

Three Heckler and Koch MP5SFs and two Glock 17s opened fire on the animal. Despite them not being silver bullets, they tore into his flesh, penetrated his organs. He writhed in agony and then fell to the floor.

He panted desperately and tried to get up again, but the injuries were too much. He lost consciousness and died.

To no one's surprise, the body didn't turn back into that of a man; it was just a dead wolf. Somehow it had got into the Place of Safety and killed a nurse, and the patient who was also known to have been there was never found. The investigation was swift and silent. No one went to court and it never appeared in the media.

The true and short life of a werewolf.

A STOPOVER IN BURDEN

Adena Graham

Once, many years ago, there existed a place called Burden. It was located somewhere between Here and There – although, for the most part, it resided in the territory of Nowhere. Its dark capital crouched like a small, cancerous mass amid a populace ground down by discontent and bitterness. Its urban fingers sprawled briefly outwards, until they seemed to forget their purpose, give up, and give way to parched fields and spindly trees.

These hinterlands were known as Despair, and a half-hearted river crawled through them, carving out a feeble tributary that looked as though it might vanish, given the right climatic conditions.

It was into Burden that a man named Saul Ohio rode late one night. His horse, grown lame a number of miles back, had rallied, bringing him to the doors of a large, shabby inn, before collapsing and exhaling its last breath into the dustbowl that was Main Street.

Saul took one parting look at his faithful nag, then pushed his way through the entranceway of Burden Inn, where he approached the sullen, moustachioed clerk who was manning reception.

Although the reception area was devoid of any other patrons, the clerk displayed no visible sign of interest on finding a potentially paying guest standing before him. Indeed, he barely raised his eyes from the game of Solitaire he was playing, giving Ohio a quick glance up and down before mumbling, 'How can I assist you?'

'I'd like a room for the night. Maybe two nights, if you have one going,' Saul said. From the look of the place, he reckoned he could have the run of the establishment for a year without encountering many other folk.

The clerk made a show of checking his ledger, trailing a stubby finger across the lines of the book. 'Could squeeze you in for one night. Not sure about two, though.'

'Gets busy here, does it?' Saul asked, seeing nothing but blank space taking up the pages of the tome.

'Not busy in the way you might think,' the clerk replied, finally meeting Saul's eye and holding his gaze.

'Busy how, then?'

'Ah, well you'd be surprised how things turn around here. One night nobody, next night nobody, and so on and so on. But then there are times when we enjoy a fair flurry of visitors. Might not look it, but we're a popular stopping-off point. Take your own self for example, sir. Whatever the purpose of your visit to Burden, I'm willing to lay money on the fact that your business isn't here, in this town. Maybe it's a ways down the road. Maybe it's in the next city. Whatever your agenda, I'm guessing you weren't planning on stopping off here.'

Saul took a deep breath, feeling the weariness flood into his bones. 'You're right. I'll own that this town was not my destination. Not tonight, sir, nor any night. But my horse grew lame and I was hoping to rest him up here awhile before continuing on.'

The clerk did a double take and made a show of looking around. 'So where is this fine, albeit lame, beast, sir? We have a serviceable if shabby stables around back. I can call on our stable hand to indulge your horse with enough hay and water to make him comfortable. Him being a horse, I'm sure he won't mind that those equine premises have seen better days.'

Saul held up a hand. 'That won't be necessary. Unfortunately, your locale was a mile too much for my gelding. He collapsed outside. He is there now, nose to the dust. I expect I will need someone to come and take him to wherever it is you bury your departed steeds around here.'

The clerk, raising a finger, dabbed at the corner of both eyes, in a show of mock sadness. 'Oh, sorry to hear that, sir. Very sorry. And so it begins.'

'So what begins?' Saul asked, raising an eyebrow.

'Why, so begins your purpose in Burden.'

'I don't follow. As I said, I have no purpose here, other than a stopover. I shall be gone in the morning – the next at the very latest.'

'Yes, I'm sure you expect that you will,' murmured the clerk. 'Until then, here is your key. Room six. Up the stairs, third door on the left. I hope all will be to your liking, but if it isn't, please don't feel that I'll be able to do much about it. Good night, sir. And good luck.'

* * *

As Saul ascended the stairs, he wondered at the strange turn the conversation had taken, and resolved to quiz the clerk further in the morning. For now, though, he concentrated on turning the key to room six, which had become stuck and was refusing to cooperate. After a few more tweaks and shoves, the lock finally gave way, revealing a small, dour room that had nothing to recommend it in the slightest, apart from the fact that it was a room and provided some shelter at least.

A sagging, narrow bed sat in one corner, opposite a small washbasin that was chipped and cracked with age, its once-white surface rimmed with grime from others' ablutions. A single wardrobe took up the other corner and, next to it, a decrepit chest of drawers.

It was a monk's quarters, but without the requisite sense of peace. Quite the contrary. This room had a heavy, oppressive feel and, all at once, Saul felt a sense of doom descend upon him. He immediately set to whistling, but no tune, however jolly, could ease the creeping dread that layered itself thickly about his person and which grew more profound with each passing minute.

Shedding his clothes, down to his long johns, Saul crawled into the cold, uninviting bed, where he lay, passing the lengthy hours until dawn, trying to ward off the growing instinct that something was amiss inside the Burden Inn.

* * *

The next morning, finding the front desk empty, Saul made his way towards the rear of the establishment, in search of breakfast. After a few wrong turns, he eventually stumbled across a shabby parlour. The heavy curtains were still drawn, and Saul's eyes took a moment or two to adjust to the gloom. Through this veil of murky light, he estimated there were around twelve empty tables to choose from, but since only one was laid, it was at this table he settled himself.

The silence within the room soon became something tangible and heavy. All of the usual bustling, tinkling, clattering sounds of morning at an inn were absent, and Saul was just about to retreat and hunt down breakfast elsewhere in Burden when a waiter appeared, shuffling through a set of swing doors at the back of the room. It was the clerk from the previous night.

'Oh, so you wait too?' Saul said.

'Too? I don't know what else I may be called upon to do here, sir,' the clerk/waiter replied, 'but if it should be anything more than waiting these tables, nobody has told me about it.'

'But I saw you last night. You were overseeing the reception desk.'

'No, not I.'

Saul could feel his temper rising. 'You did indeed. We spoke about my horse – it had collapsed on the way into Burden.'

'I'm sorry to hear that, sir. This is not uncommon. Most horses do expire in this manner.'

'What is this charade, man?' Saul yelled, thumping his fist on the table. 'Tell me, do you have a twin?'

'Not that I know of,' the waiter replied, his moustache twitching.

'Well, a doppelganger of any sort?'

'I couldn't say. But not here. Now, what may I bring

you for breakfast? Our eggs are mainly scrambled, no matter how else you wish them to be, and our toast is invariably burnt, but things only get worse from here on in, so I'd make the most of them if I were you.'

The waiter made to retreat, but Saul stood quickly, his chair clattering to the floor, and grabbed him by the arm. 'I demand you explain what's going on here. This inn isn't normal. Not by any stretch.'

'Very perceptive of you to notice, sir.'

'No wonder nobody wants to stay here. It's a shambles.'

'I wouldn't say that. We're full to capacity at the moment, sir. Very popular if you ask me.'

Saul took a deep breath, attempting to steady his nerves. 'But last night I saw your ledger. It was devoid of names. This tavern is quiet as the grave. There is nobody else here but I, it would seem. What game are you playing with me?'

'You are here, but not yet looking,' the waiter said, his lips rising in the semblance of a smile, his eyes as cold as a snake's.

Instinctively, Saul raised his own eyes, letting them roam briefly around the room. As he did so, he caught a movement in his peripheral vision, a dark shadow in the region of the table next to his. Turning, he saw more shadows form, just out of his immediate sightline.

'Your companions,' said the waiter. 'Can I get you some coffee while you wait?'

'I shan't be waiting for anything. My business here is concluded,' Saul hissed.

Gritting his teeth, he strode out of the parlour, towards the lobby. The way wasn't right, though. At every turn, the passages confounded him, until he found himself come full circle, back outside the parlour.

The waiter was immediately before him, grinning wolfishly. 'You'll find there isn't a way out of Burden, sir. Not until it's time for you to go on to Despair, at least. We're just waiting for one more guest to join you and the others, then you can all head on over together.'

'Others?' Saul shouted, feeling tears course down his cheeks. His sight blurred, and he suddenly saw, with full clarity of vision, what he'd hitherto been unable to. There, at the other tables and chairs, the shadowy forms of people began to reveal themselves. A man and a woman at one were clutching hands and weeping. Next to them, a waitress poured coffee into two chipped, dirty mugs.

Across the room, a man was hugging himself, rocking to and fro. At another table, a priest sat, his hands clasped together in silent prayer, his lips soundlessly reciting an entreaty that the Almighty was clearly ignoring. Beyond them, at a corner table, a wan-faced woman raised the back of her hand to her brow, exposing a cross-hatch of scars blighting the alabaster skin upon her wrist.

And there were more besides. Whichever way Saul turned, another face appeared out of the shadows – each bearing an expression more hopeless than the last.

'Your travelling companions, sir,' the waiter said. 'Each of you entered Burden during this past week, and soon you will leave. We are, as I'm sure you were told, just a stopping-off point.'

'Goddamn my horse!' Saul snapped. 'If that godforsaken beast hadn't lamed itself then died, I could have passed by here and escaped these games.'

The waiter chuckled. 'Oh, sir, it's not your horse that

was godforsaken. Not a bit of it. Wasn't just your horse that died either.'

Trembling, Saul fell to his knees. 'You lie! You lie, man! I am clearly very much alive. I'm as alive as you. I am. Here, I pinch myself and it hurts. I am flesh and blood, and you are toying with me in a most grotesque way.'

'Ah, sir, it's been a long time since I was alive,' the waiter murmured. 'Here in Burden is my Purgatory. Look and see.'

Raising his eyes, Saul let out a choked gasp. Before him, the waiter had transformed into nothing more than smoke and shadow. 'I must go now, there are more guests arriving soon,' it whispered, its voice now thin and insubstantial. 'There are always more guests arriving at Burden. Always more.'

'Wait,' Saul gasped. 'Don't go. I need to know. Just one more thing. You said Burden is a stopping-off point for us. A stopping-off point for where?'

'Why, Hell, sir,' came the voice, fainter now, a mere memory of sound. 'And once you see Despair, you'll realise quite how lovely your stay here in Burden has been.'

INFESTATION

Jennifer Jackson

<u>Then:</u>

First, there were ants. Scuttling all over the once white galley-style kitchen. Their teamwork moving in a black sea of tidal rhythms. All the surfaces and most of the floor were covered with plates, cups and cutlery, which the ants were submerging. I wanted to move but my body wouldn't let me.

The only visible plate was the one with brownish red cemented onto it with a coat of bluish-white fur. It must have once been leftover tomato ketchup. Every cup contained a furry gloop of rainbow mould. It gave the room a chemical, rotten tang which burnt my nostrils and the back of my throat. It reminded me of the time when my mum made me sandwiches for my packed lunch. This smelt just like the acidic smog that hit the roof of my mouth before I saw the bluish green pierced with my own teeth marks. That was the only time that my mum could put down the vodka for long enough to make me a packed lunch.

Muffled whispers jolted me back to the present. *For God's sake Tammy, that was twenty years ago. Let it go, you silly bitch!* Just as I batted the memory away, I heard the whispering again. Then a pause just long enough to wonder if I'd imagined it.

'Little Miss "Won't Turn Out Like My Mother" eh? Ha! Pathetic!' a woman's voice spat at me.

No, this wasn't a flashback. This voice was definitely too gravelly to belong to the childhood friends who turned against me and used to follow me home with whispers, taunts and cackles. A low, raucous laugh dripped with malice, and then fell silent just as suddenly. I felt like a kitten being picked up by the scruff of the neck.

Before I could respond, my attention was drawn downwards as I saw my blue sock awash with the tide. My scream reverberated around the house as I ripped off my sock, threw it onto a black crest of ants in the corner, closed the kitchen door and ran up the stairs as far away from it as possible.

The journey upstairs was an assault course of dirty laundry and more crockery. I had to hold onto the banisters to steady myself since there was no visible carpet.

I rushed to my bedroom, closed the door, stepped over yet more packets, clothes and plates, and sank under the sanctuary of my formerly crisp white, now dank grey, bedding. Lying on the matted grease of my hair felt like an extra pillow. I couldn't remember the last time that my hair was clean and my teeth weren't caked in a brown glue of plaque. Occasionally I got a waft of my own foul odour. The sweat of each day piled on top of each other, curdled with the eye-wateringly sour, urine-tinted stench of unwashed vagina. As was my only hobby of late, I buried myself under the duvet. I was safe in there. Or rather, everyone else was safe.

I couldn't leave the house without having to repeat the journey over and over in case there was a blank in my memory where I'd hurt someone. The last time that I went out, I was waiting to cross the road, when I had a sudden impulse to throw the frail old lady next to me into the traffic. I had to follow her home to check that I hadn't done that, and I had to keep counting my steps to erase the thoughts. There are 150 steps between the traffic lights and her house.

I don't know how many hours had passed, but there was now not enough daylight to lighten the room. I hadn't heard anything since going upstairs. I needed to clear up as much as I could and then ring Pest Control. After sitting decisively upright, I almost tripped over myself in determination as I gathered plates and packets on my way to the kitchen. There had been at least three seasons since the last time that I had done any tidying. I grabbed a bin bag that was bulging out of the cupboard under the stairs and shoved things into it. When I yanked open the kitchen door, I looked everywhere except the floor as I made sweeping motions to get everything, living or dead, in the bin bag. My periphery startled me with the absence of blackness. *Where had they all gone?* It was even darker outside when I emerged from my standstill of bewilderment. Shrugging in conclusion, I slung the bulging bin bag outside the back door, before crawling with exhaustion back to bed.

I had several nights of undisturbed sleep, despite having not moved from the bed other than to go to the toilet and to eat meals from paper plates with plastic cutlery that didn't need washing. I had decided that the woman's voice must have been coming from the kitchen since that's where it was loudest. In the bedroom, it had reduced to decibels that I could ignore. The only safe space was the bed. Until it wasn't.

I woke up to something moving under the skin of my arms. I tried sleepily scratching away the itch, but it made no difference. I turned on the light. Parts of skin stretched and then sagged back into place to accommodate the long and thin wriggling bulges. There were so many of them, writhing around in zig zags of uncoordinated sync. The itch slithered from my armpits right to the tips of my fingers. I ran downstairs to find a knife to cut them out.

Luckily there was a clean one in the drawer. The sting of the blade and the tearing of skin as I reached in to pull them out offered no relief. I couldn't reach the worms. One of the cuts started to slowly dribble a warm, thick black-red.

I woozily dialled 999. *Worms in skin… No, not fucking scabies! …Worms in my skin… Cuts…. Bleeding…. Lots of …bleeding.*

"If you're telling me that you've cut yourself deliberately, I'm going to have to send an ambulance over to you. Leave the door unlocked, they're on their way." Her utterly inconvenienced sigh and nasal condescension are the last memory I have before being in unbearable brightness.

I wanted to shield my eyes under the pathetic blanket rather than talk to the wan-looking ferret of a man with his pen and clipboard. He wasn't listening to me. His sing-song voice was almost as irritating as the wriggling in my skin. I gasped as I felt tugging underneath my stitches, and my stomach churned as I saw my skin becoming increasingly concave with each worm's pull of each thread. The man was completely indifferent as this evening's Pot Noodle cascaded onto my lap through a waterfall of stomach acid. I could barely breathe between wailing and retching.

'Get them out of me!' I pleaded breathlessly, gesturing at each of my desperately flailing arms.

He remained impassive. Jotting notes. Staring through me like I was a boring PowerPoint presentation. More notes. Scribble, scribble, scribble. *Why did he have to press his pen down so hard?* The deafening scratching on the paper and the worms writhing and pulling made me shudder and press my hands to my ears.

'Stop it! Just listen to me! Please! Just…'

No. It couldn't be. The malicious, smoker's laugh sent a jolt of startled electricity through me. *She must have followed me from the house.* A woman of about forty or so kept skipping around the room. *It must be her. How dare this waif-like strip of piss, torment me?*

'What do you want?' I shrieked. She didn't even look up. Fury scratched my throat with each yell as I leapt off the bed and lunged towards her. Just before I could grab her hair and throw a fist, I was face-down on the floor with knees crushing my back and vice-like hands on my head and around my arms and legs. A metallic warmth hit my tongue as a little finger crunched between my teeth and the adjoining hand let go with a yelp. I felt a jab in my left buttock. The severed finger dribbled out of my mouth as everything turned black.

I don't know exactly how long I was in hospital for. It was a dream-like haze. Upon getting home, my only welcome was the mountains of unopened bills and mouldy plates. I couldn't even remember the last time that I had received a text. I used to have a best friend called Laura. She ghosted me, until I kept begging her for answers. She relented, and told me that my constant asking her if I had hurt anyone on every outing, drunk or sober, was too much for her. I couldn't trust anyone else. Sighing, I ignored the letters and the crockery and trudged upstairs to bed.

The next few days, possibly weeks, were spent in bed watching Netflix and falling in and out of sleep, too drowsy to appreciate each punchline or twist, but welcoming the familiarity of the activity. One day, I realised that I'd run out of medication, but I was too exhausted to go and get some more. Besides, I was even more unable to leave the house. My bras didn't even cover one third of each breast, and my feet and ankles were too swollen to fit into what used to be my most comfortable trainers.

One inert day yawned into the next on a repeat cycle. I didn't do anything but sleep, eat and go to the toilet. That was until I woke up drowning in my own sweat, pulling my hair and slapping my head after a dream about seeing naked children giggling and chasing each other on the beach, joyously in the moment, and me being frozen in motion, unable to turn my head like I wanted to.

'You sick nonce!' The woman's smoky northern gravel, like scraping phlegm-filled lungs on a cheese grater, catapulted me awake. I got up and looked under the bed, in the wardrobe, everywhere that I could think of in my palpitating state. As I opened my bedroom door, the word 'paedophile' smacked me in the face in big letters on the wall opposite the door, written in blood from a new cut on my forearm that I didn't remember making. I gasped, inhaling metallic rust as I put my hand to my mouth. The brownish-red still on the fingers that I didn't remember writing with.

I frantically searched the house for this woman. Ripping open every door and all the curtains, tipping over the sofa and chairs, exposing all hiding places. None of which exposed her.

Who was she?

How could she have seen my dream?

Why couldn't I look away?

Oh God! Does that mean that I wanted to look?

I had never been attracted to children, but bile burned the back of my throat at the idea that I could do the worst possible thing. I had always thought that castration, or even the death penalty, was the only option for such monsters. I certainly wouldn't make any exceptions for myself.

I had to run to the bathroom as the acid came rushing to the tip of my mouth. I had to try not to choke while crying over the toilet basin. As I stood up and wiped my mouth on my sleeve, I caught a glimpse of the overflowing bin. *Shit! I didn't have any more socks or magazine pages.*

'Ha! You can't even buy enough toilet roll *and* you're a dirty nonce! Pathetic! There's only one thing that scum like you should do!'

The sheer venom trickled down my spine.

A screaming baby and a mother making desperate yet futile attempts to soothe it walked underneath the window. The panic smothered me.

'Don't bother with that counting crap. We both know that you can feel your cunt tingling, you dirty nonce!'

I was about to protest. Then I did feel it. I crossed my legs, squeezing in repulsion.

My next memory is of being in the bathroom sitting in a pool of blood. A knife drowning in the pool a few centimetres away from my hand.

Now:

I've been on the Bracken psychiatric ward for six months now.

I can't get into a comfortable position. It feels like there's a huge rock in my stomach with my bowels twisting in protest. Rubbing it takes the pain from a ten to a nine-point-nine. Ferret man, AKA Dr Graham, sits on the chair to the left of my bed. His eyes are too big and too far apart for the rest of his face. His big, drooping nose and thin lips are squashed into the little space that his forehead reluctantly left a little bit of room for. That and his pointy chin make him look very rodent-like. His hair, jumper and trousers are all a tedious shade of beige.

'Hello Tammy, how are we?' That sing-song voice would be more appropriate at a children's party.

I force a smile and shrug. Anything else is too much effort.

'You're certainly more responsive than you were a few months ago,' he says with an uncomfortable and forced laugh. 'It's good to see that you're feeling a little brighter!'

He can't be serious. Surely?

'I'm not! I'm in so much pain. I'm all blocked up.'

'We can easily remedy the constipation. I'll prescribe some laxatives. Walking around the ward will also help to get things moving!' *What was he stealing from the pharmacy to make him so fucking cheerful?*

'These meds are making me feel awful. Do I really have to take them?'

'I'm afraid that I can't take you off the Olanzapine. It is vital for stopping the hallucinations. Especially since not taking it resulted in you needing a blood transfusion. We do not prescribe these medications lightly. It really is a matter of keeping you alive and safe.'

Alive, safe, up six dress sizes and with a mutilated vulva, I want to say but don't. Who knew that I wouldn't be the only one? Shelley, who's currently walking around in a post-sedation stupor, is always finding new ways to stab herself there. She even used a plastic fork a few weeks ago.

'You have been far more lucid recently, and there have been no documented incidents of self-harm or violent attacks for a few months now. Providing that you keep taking your medication…'

He numbers each requirement with his fingers as he speaks.

'…you stay in an outpatient hostel for at least six months, you have daily sessions with the crisis team for at least six weeks, and that you have therapy with Dr Burnett, a specialist in Obsessive Compulsive Disorder and psychosis, we can make plans to discharge you in the coming weeks.'

The taste of freedom is interrupted by heavy breathing and grunts from Maggie in the next bed. The curtain hides nothing.

'Right… ahem…' Dr Graham coughs awkwardly with flushed cheeks. Bundling up his notes clumsily, he stands up.

'It'll be the medication round in a minute, so I'll… ahem… erm… leave you to it.'

Her or me? I want to ask. I snigger to myself and pick up my journal.

For about an hour, there's only the page, the pen and me. Until I am brought back to the external environment by animated and slightly heated conversation coming from the staff room. As though they are talking *about* rather than *to* the offending person. I'm not normally a gossip, but I find myself straining to hear who they are talking about.

'Oh my God that's awful! What a sicko! Life should mean life for scum like that. Our justice system is so broken.' I hear Sarah – the usually softly spoken Nurse Atkinson – sounding more outraged than I have ever heard her sound. Hers is the only voice that I can recognise.

I'm intrigued.

'Yeah, I know. There's only one thing that scum like that should do.'

A fist of terror grabs my throat. That harsh gravel. I feel dizzy. I can hear my heart's frantic throb in my ears. Like swimming underwater and being desperate to swim to safety.

'Right, I'd better go and do the medication round.'

Such an ordinary sentence. So much threat.

A woman comes through the door with a blue 'medication round' pinafore on. Her thick bleached blonde hair tied back in a messy bun. She is small with hunched-over shoulders and is almost skeletally thin. Her heavy foundation and red lipstick fail miserably to disguise the bags and wrinkles under and around her eyes and the smoker's wrinkles around her lips. She looks so haggard and frail. She couldn't scare a small child in the dark. I remind myself of this as she edges towards my bed. Every movement clearly takes momentous effort and energy. I feel the fear melt away from me. I even pity her.

As she reaches my bed, she puts a band around my bicep before placing a test tube above the needle. Nothing out of the ordinary. My blood needs to be tested regularly. Sharp scratch. Deep breaths. All done.

Why hasn't she taken the band off my arm? What is she drawing up?

I feel a sharp pain.

'Time for sleep.'

A spiteful smile accompanies the hoarse menace that only I can notice.

I start itching all over. An ant crawls from the needle into the injection hole and joins a scattering of others under my skin. Pitter-pattering all the way up my arm and around my body. I'm shaking and feel froth coming out of my mouth. I can't move or speak but I can hear, see and feel everything.

She starts coughing uncontrollably. Right from the bottom of her lungs. Holding onto my bed. Her face red with the exertion. A black tidal wave cascades out of her mouth and all over me. They set to work immediately. Crawling up my nose, down both ears, down my throat and into my eyes. Everything itching. Blackness dancing on my eyeballs. Unable to scratch away the itch. Until I feel, hear and see nothing.

AUTHOR BIOGRAPHIES

These are printed in alphabetical order by contributor surname.

C.C. Adams

London native C.C. Adams is the horror/dark fiction author behind books such as *But Worse Will Come*, *Forfeit Tissue* and *There Goes Pretty*. A member of the Horror Writers Association, he still lives in the capital. This is where he lifts weights, cooks – and looks for the perfect quote to set off the next dark delicacy.

Cathy Bryant

Cathy Bryant has won 30 literary awards and writing contests, including the Wergle Flomp Humorous Poetry Contest, the Balticon SF Poetry Contest and the Bulwer-Lytton Fiction Contest. Cathy's work has been published all over the world in such publications as *Eye to the Telescope*, *The Andromeda Spaceways Inflight Magazine* and *Futuredaze*. She co-edited the anthologies *Best of Manchester Poets vols. 1, 2 and 3* and has had three books of poetry published: *Contains Strong Language and Scenes of a Sexual Nature* (Puppywolf, 2010), *Look at All the Women* (Mother's Milk, 2014) and *Erratics* (Arachne, 2018).

Justin Cawthorne

Justin Cawthorne is interested in creating tales that explore new ways to draw terror from both the known and unknown. In partnership with the *Tales to Terrify* podcast, he has received a Parsec Award for Best Speculative Fiction Story: Small Cast (Short Form) for the adaptation of his story "Graves". His other work in speculative fiction includes his novella *There Is a Light That Never Goes Out* and the short story "Colder Still" which appears in the Darkwater Syndicate anthology *Shadows and Teeth*.

Sue Eaton

As a girl growing up in Northamptonshire, Sue Eaton became fascinated by the work of authors such as Ray Bradbury, John Wyndham and Terry Nation, developing a lifelong love for a well-written psychological horror story. She worked for many years as a teacher of children with autism. Her writing is now one of her major passions. She has had her work broadcast on BBC Radio 4. Her debut novel, *The Woman Who Was Not His Wife*, was published in 2018, followed by the novella *The Boyfriend* in 2021. As Sue J. Eaton, she is also the editor of *The Corona Book of Ghost Stories*.

Jon Gauthier

Jon Gauthier is a part-time horror, sci-fi and thriller writer from Ottawa, Ontario, Canada. Jon says he's been in love with storytelling ever since he saw *Jurassic Park* at the age of eight and has been writing his own stories ever since he discovered the *Goosebumps* and *Scary Stories to Tell in the Dark* books only a year after that. His work has appeared in many publications, including most recently *Etherea Magazine* and the Cemetery Gates Media anthology *Campfire Macabre*. He counts Richard Matheson, Stephen

King, Brian Keene, Joe Hill, Jonathan Janz, and Hunter Shea among his major influences.

Adena Graham

Adena Graham is a copywriter by day, writer by night. As a copywriter, she's created ads and written copy for a wide variety of household names, including the likes of British Airways, L'Oreal, Nissan, Wendy's, Tesco, and Marks & Spencer. As a writer, she has had numerous short stories published both online and in various literary magazines, including *Unhinged, Dead Things, QWF, Midnight Street, Writers' Brew, Faber Quickfic* and the acclaimed magazine *Popshot Quarterly*. She's also had two erotic novels published under a pen name (which name she won't be revealing to her mother any time soon, no matter how many times she asks her to!)

Donna L. Greenwood

Donna L Greenwood writes flash fiction, short stories and poetry. Her work has been nominated for Best Small Fictions, Best Microfiction and a Pushcart Prize. Her debut novelette-in-flash "The Impossibility of Wings" has recently been published by Retreat West. She is currently working on a horror novella and short story collection.

Jennifer Jackson

"Infestation" is Jennifer Jackson's first published story and a result of her having started to take her lifelong dream of being a writer seriously at the age of 30, following a mental and physical breakdown. Despite being told at school that she "wasn't academic" due to her "special needs", Jennifer has degrees in Philosophy, Theology and Religious Studies, and has had all sorts of jobs, including temping as a postal worker but constantly getting lost. She has autism and M.E., identifies as queer, and fights mental health demons. Online she can be found ranting, and cuddling and walking her goonish Labrador and German Shepherd on Instagram at @jenandvincerant.

Suzanne Ross Jones

Suzanne Ross Jones is a writer of short stories and romance (who also writes under the name Suzanna Ross). Her pocket novels have been published in the UK by DC Thomson and her books, which have been published by Linford Romance, are available from libraries. Her short stories and serials have been published in magazines in the UK and Australia. She lives in Scotland where she dreams of being rich and building a house in the country overlooking a picturesque loch away from noise. She dislikes intensely people who drive too close with no respect for stopping distances. She loves her family and lime creams.

Florence Ann Marlowe

Florence Ann Marlowe is an active member of the Horror Writers Association and the Masters of Horror Community. Her stories have been published in numerous collections and anthologies including *Deadman's Tome*, *Trumpocalypse*, *Fear's Accomplice*, *Black Candies* and *Man Behind the Mask*. Born and raised in Hoboken,

Florence has lived from one end of New Jersey to the other. She currently lives in the same neighbourhood where the legendary Jersey Devil is said to have been born. Rumour has it, he lives next door.

Sam Rebelein

Sam Rebelein holds an MFA in Creative Writing from Goddard College, with a focus on Horror and Memoir. Before that, he graduated with a BA in English and Education from Vassar College. Sam's work has appeared in speculative fiction magazines – including *Bourbon Penn, Planet Scumm, Dark Moon Digest* and *Shimmer* – as well as in Ellen Datlow's prestigious *Best Horror of the Year*. His story "Black-Fanged Thing" was listed as a stand-out piece of 2018 on Barnes & Noble's *Sci-fi & Fantasy Blog*. HarperCollins' horror and crime imprint William Morrow will publish Sam's debut horror novel *Edenville* in 2023, and his debut short story collection *The Poorly Made and Other Things* in 2024.

Vanessa Reid

Vanessa Reid is a dark fiction writer and an English teacher in Atlanta. When she is not making her sixth-graders watch *The Twilight Zone* and read Poe, she writes about the human monsters that haunt us. Her story "The Short Straw" was recently featured in *Gutwrench Journal*. She is a member of the Broadleaf Writers Association and the Horror Writers Association, where she is the Atlanta chapter treasurer. Reid lives with her adorably macabre family, an evil cat named Moreland, and a dog who is just trying to avoid his wrath.

MM Schreier

MM Schreier is a classically trained vocalist who took up writing as therapy for a mid-life crisis. Whether contemporary or speculative fiction, favourite stories are dark and rich in sensory details. A firm believer that people are not always exclusively right- or left-brained, in addition to creative pursuits, Schreier manages a robotics company and tutors maths and science to at-risk youth. After years of finding the muse in the mountains, Schreier and a very spoiled Labrador Retriever have inched a bit south to see what the beach might inspire.

The Secret Submissive

The Secret Submissive is a British Indian writer of honest and immersive BDSM erotica. She is the author of the *A Taste of Submission* and *Fantasies* book series, in which her stories are inspired by her own real-life experiences and desires. She is a passionate advocate for the importance of trust, equality and consent within a relationship, and her writing features healthy Dom/Sub relationships that challenge and reinvent the stereotypes of "normality". By day, she works as a secondary school English teacher and in her free time enjoys yoga, baking and binge-watching true-crime dramas.

Deborah Sheldon

Deborah Sheldon is an award-winning author from Australia. She writes short stories, novellas and novels across the darker spectrum. Award-nominated titles include *Body Farm Z*, *Contrition*, *Devil Dragon*, *Thylacines*, and *Figments and Fragments: Dark Stories*. Her collection *Perfect Little Stitches and Other Stories* won the Australian Shadows "Best Collected Work" Award and was long-listed for a Bram Stoker. She has won the Australian Shadows "Best Edited Work" Award twice: for *Midnight Echo 14* and *Spawn*. Her short fiction has appeared in prestigious magazines and "best of" anthologies. Other credits include TV scripts, feature articles, non-fiction books and award-winning medical writing.

Augustus Stephens

Augustus Stephens is a poet, musician, writer, performer and champion for mental health. He has written three one-person-shows about mental illness, largely drawn from his own experience, and performed these at Edinburgh and other fringes garnering five-star reviews. He also writes comic songs and has two solo albums available online or on CD. He loves the outdoors but can't stand the cold, so whilst most of the year he's tucked up inside with a blanket, in summer he can be found talking to the trees and the stars dressed as nature intended. His claim to fame is being arrested on a walk with the Naked Rambler on BBC1 Television.

Wink Taylor

Wink Taylor is a voice-over artist, actor, writer and performer. He has written for national television and the West End stage, writing over 30 episodes of the *Sooty* TV series in which he also appears on screen. In print he is the author of the Doctor Who spin-off novel *The Bandril Invasion* in Candy Jar Books' The Lucy Wilson Mysteries series as well as short stories in their Lethbridge-Stewart series. As an actor he has played Winston Churchill, Kenneth Williams, Marty Feldman and even appeared in Doctor Who; and as an entertainer he has starred on stage in venues including The London Palladium, Theatre Royal Drury Lane and Birmingham's Symphony Hall.

Wondra Vanian

Wondra Vanian was a Top-Ten finisher in the Preditors and Editors Reader's Poll four years running, including in the best author category. Her story "Halloween Night" was a Notable Contender for the Bristol Short Story Prize and "It Would be a Waste" was shortlisted for the Twisted Tales Flash Fiction Competition. An American living in the UK with her husband and a mischief of sausage dogs, Wondra is an avid gamer, photographer, cinephile and blogger. She has music in her blood, sleeps with the lights on, strikes bargains with crows, and has been known to dance naked in the moonlight.

D.A. Watson

D.A. Watson is the author of four novels, *The Wolves of Langabhat* (2015), *In the Devil's Name* (2016), *Cuttin' Heads* (2018) and *Adonias Low* (2021); and the fiction and poetry collection *Tales of What the Fuck* (2019). His stories, verse and articles have also appeared in several anthologies to widespread acclaim. An occasional poetry performer, he appeared on the main stage of the Burnsfest Festival in 2018 as the warm-up act for the one and only Chesney Hawkes, a personal milestone and career highlight. He lives with his family on the west coast of Scotland and is still telling stories.

Lewis Williams

Lewis Williams founded Corona Books UK in 2015. His literary endeavours have been multifarious. As well as being the editor of and occasional contributor to all four volumes of the *Corona Book of Horror Stories*, his writing has covered areas as diverse as social policy, music and humour. Lewis has been – or still is – many things including an author, editor, publisher, Philosophy graduate, higher-education administrator, researcher for Oxford University, buyer of parts for industrial robots, local government officer, property developer, and part-qualified electrician. Maybe he should get a grip.

AUTHOR WEBSITES AND TWITTER ACCOUNTS

Those authors who have Twitter accounts and/or websites are listed below.

C.C. Adams
Twitter: @MrAdamsWrites
website: ccadams.com

Cathy Bryant
website: compsandcalls.com/wp

Justin Cawthorne
Twitter: @SlightlyOddTale
website: justincawthorne.com

Sue Eaton
Twitter: @SueJayEaton
website: susanjeaton.com

Jon Gauthier
Twitter: @JAGaut
website: jgauthier.ca

Adena Graham
website: adenagraham1.wixsite.com/fiction

Donna L. Greenwood
Twitter: @DonnaLouise67
website: thehorrorsblog.wordpress.com

Jennifer Jackson

website: jenniferjacksonwriting.uk

Suzanne Ross Jones

Twitter: @sj_suz

Florence Ann Marlowe

Twitter: @FAMarlowe

Sam Rebelein

Twitter: @HillaryScruff
website: srebelein.com

Vanessa Reid

Twitter: @vhowrenreid
website: vanessareidfiction.wordpress.com

MM Schreier

Twitter: @NoD1v1ng
website: mmschreier.com

The Secret Submissive

Twitter: @TSubmissive
website: thesecretsubmissive.com

Deborah Sheldon

website: deborahsheldon.wordpress.com

Augustus Stephens

Twitter: @AugustusNDS
website: augustusemperors.com

Wink Taylor
Twitter: @WinkTaylor1

Wondra Vanian
Twitter: @wondravanian
website: wondravanian.com

D.A. Watson
Twitter   @davewatsonbooks
website: dawatsonwriter.com

Lewis Williams
website: lewiswilliams.com

Independent Publishers of the
Best in New Genre Short Fiction (and More)

Corona Books UK was established in 2015. Our primary focus is on publishing the best new short stories in horror, sci-fi and speculative fiction.

For the latest on other titles published by us and forthcoming attractions, please visit our website and follow us on Twitter.

www.coronabooks.com

@CoronaBooksUK

Readers of this book may also be interested in checking out *The Corona Book of Horror Stories*, *The Second Corona Book of Horror Stories*, *The Third Corona Book of Horror Stories* and *The Corona Book of Ghost Stories*. Readers, in particular who enjoyed the stories by MM Schreier or Sue Eaton in this book, may also be interested in *The Corona Book of Science Fiction*, which includes stories from these two authors amongst other great sci-fi short stories.